Carroll

MORGAN'S LEAP BOOK 1

KATHI S. BARTON

This is a work of fiction. Names, characters, places, and incidents are products of the author's imagination or are used fictitiously and are not to be construed as real. Any resemblance to actual events, locations, organizations, or persons, living or dead, is entirely coincidental.

World Castle Publishing, LLC
Pensacola, Florida
Copyright © Kathi S. Barton 2021
Paperback ISBN: 9781953271877
eBook ISBN: 9781953271884
First Edition World Castle Publishing, LLC, March 8, 2021
http://www.worldcastlepublishing.com
Licensing Notes
Cover: Karen Fuller
Editor: Maxine Bringenberg

Prologue

Morgan made herself into a tight ball as she hid herself in the tall grasses in the field. She knew the men chasing her would find her soon enough, but for now, she was going to make them work for it. Closing her eyes, trying her best to calm her breathing, she did the only thing she could to not think about what was going on around her. Morgan counted to fifty in all the languages she knew.

She had awakened out here. All she remembered was having dinner in the kitchen with the staff and then waking out in the middle of the moonless night. She did not remember going to bed or putting on the nightgown she had on now. Nor did she remember waking when brought out here in the cool night. Soon after waking, she heard the voices of the men, six she thought she'd counted, saying the first one that found her could have her. At fourteen, Morgan knew exactly what that meant. They were going to rape her, then more than likely kill her.

Her parents would be looking for her. She would admit, only to herself, that they'd not be too upset about her being gone. Morgan had a habit of getting up in the middle of the night to see to one creature or another. So it might be days before anyone—

The hot breath of air on her forehead had her whimper just a little. Lifting her head without opening her eyes, she felt it once again. It was hot but not sour-smelling. Opening her eyes, she looked right into the golden eyes of a leopard. Their noses touched. They were so close.

The lick to her face scared her. While she'd seen the wild animals around the compound where she lived, she'd never been this close to one so dangerous. The farmers would kill them when they would take down a cow or something they raised, but no one could have prepared her for their beauty being this close.

The big cat put her paw on her head and pushed it back down, so it rested on the dirt. When she started to lift it again, the cat pushed her down again. Understanding that she was to stay where she was, Morgan closed her eyes. If she was going to be eaten, she was glad the cat was sparing her from knowing when it was coming.

The sound, soft as a coin dropping onto the dusty

ground, was all she heard before the large cat screamed. There was gunfire too. Something frighteningly close stirred up some of the dirt she was hiding on. The screaming of men was next. It wasn't long before it was quiet, and she knew on some level that the cat had killed the men. The paw to her head again had her lifting it up to see if she was next.

The cat had been hurt. Blood was pouring from her shoulder at an alarming rate. Sitting up, unmindful of whether it was safe to do so, Morgan tore at her nightgown to staunch the blood as she spoke to the leopard.

"I think you saved me." The cat just let her poke around at her wound, soon lying down when she asked her to do so. "The bullet needs to come out. If it doesn't, I'm afraid you'll get sick and die from it. I wish I had my knife here. But I think I can see it enough to get it out with my fingers. I won't do any more than I have to. All right?"

Morgan worked for fifteen minutes in getting the bullet out. The cat never hurt her. Never tried to get away from her as she worked. Sweat poured off Morgan's forehead as she finally got it free. When she was finished, she showed it to the cat.

"See? Someone got a shot in. I promise you, I'll make sure you're all right. Do you have a lair? Someplace you can rest?" The cat stood up, and that was when she noticed she'd had kittens recently. "Oh no. Where are they? You left your den to come to save me? Come on. I'll help you back."

It wasn't far, only about a hundred yards from where the cat had come to her. It occurred to her that the cat was more than likely saving her kittens from being found when she killed the men, but Morgan was ever so grateful she'd spared her. Helping the cat into the den, she saw that she had three of the pudgiest little kittens she'd ever seen.

"They're beautiful. Oh, look at them. You are a good momma, Golden Eyes. They're very fat. I'll stay with you until you need to eat again. Then I'll hunt for you." The cat didn't seem to mind when Morgan picked one of the kittens up, so she touched each of them in turn. "You're very lucky those men didn't find you too. But I guess you knew that."

She stayed with the family overnight. There wasn't any way she'd be able to make her way back home in the darkness, so it was fine with her to be in the cave for the night. The kittens woke hungry a couple of times in the night. Instead of having Golden go to them, Morgan carried them back and forth to their mother. She seemed to be all right with her helping that way.

When the sun was coming up, Morgan not only made sure the family had water, but she also scavenged as much as she could from the horses the men had come out here on. Hardtack was in abundance, but she was also able to get herself some much needed flint, as well as some blankets.

Taking it to the cave, she put the kittens on one of the blankets and then sat down to watch them fall over each other until they had their spot picked out. It was calming to watch them, she thought. They were just too little to do much more than be roly-poly little kittens.

Giving the hardtack to Golden, she made her way to her home. It was further than she'd thought it might have been, and she didn't arrive there until the sun was nearly down. Going into the house by way of climbing up the back stairs, she heard her parents speaking from their balcony. Sliding out onto her own, she stood deep in the shadows to listen to what they might be saying. Her mother was standing at the railing, her father deeper in the room.

"I cannot believe she's gone." Morgan started forward, wanting to assure her mother she hadn't been hurt at all. "This was a brilliant idea you had, Malcomb. To have it look as if she'd been kidnapped, then killed. I have never wanted anything more than that child dead."

Her heart hurt. Her mind didn't know how this was really what her mother was saying. They weren't close, but she never thought she'd want her dead. But when her dad came out to the balcony too, she watched the two of them as they stood there in an embrace.

"Well, it wasn't nearly as hard as I thought it would be to get some men gathered up to take her. As you said, it's a good thing now that she's gone. When they find her body, it will be blamed on anything but me." Mother said it wouldn't be her fault either. "No. No one will bother with blaming you, my dear. For all they know, you've committed suicide because your daughter is gone."

It took her less time than it apparently did her mother to understand what her father was saying. As soon as he nearly pushed her mother over the railing, intending, she was sure, to make it look as if she had fallen to her death by her own hand, Mother grabbed her father's coat.

The two of them hung there for what seemed like forever. Would they both fall? Would they be able to save one another? She didn't care. So when her mother's weight took them both over the edge, Morgan stood there for several minutes, thinking about what had just befallen her family. Looking over the edge of her own balcony, she saw them there, tightly embraced as if in a lover's hug and dead. Blood spread out beneath their heads as if a bucket of it had been poured over the two of them.

Making her way to the kitchen area, she staggered twice in her grief. Not that they were dead — no, it was that they had planned her demise in such a cold way. Lincoln was there, the butler of the house when she entered. He took one look at her and sat her in the chair she'd spent more time in than the ones in the formal dining room. Lincoln, she knew, would be her family from now on.

"Child, what is it?" She must have been a mess. Or looked on edge. The slap to her cheek stung enough that she was brought out of whatever thoughts she'd been having. "What's happened? Your parents, they told the household you'd been kidnapped. Are you hurt?"

She told him everything, not leaving out anything, including the cat that had saved her. Also, leaving no doubt to the older man that her parents had planned for her to be killed this night. Lincoln sat down across from her after making her a cup of tea that was mostly bourbon.

"You are mistress of the house now. Tomorrow we will find their bodies whilst you are still abed. You will say you were out with the creatures of the field. They will believe that well enough. That is where you are most of the time." She asked him about the cats. "'Tis your decision. However, if you were to bring them here, none of the rest of the staff will mind. It is you we stayed for all these years, and not your parents."

"I'll need help bringing them here." He said he'd go with her. "They're far. Much further than I had thought. But I wish them to be safe, Lincoln. She saved my life, and I will do the same for her and her family."

"You have a good heart, child—a very good one. We shall leave now and take lanterns with us. A basket too so we might carry the little beasts." She asked him if he didn't want them here. "Nay, I want what you want. We all do. Tomorrow after your parents are found, we'll be as we should have been. A good home and a safe one. Mark my words on that. I will talk to you, as we go about now that you are mistress of the house, what men will do to get to you. They'll want you, but you're too stubborn to be a good wife to anyone seeking your hand. It might be well that there are cats here to protect you. You have become a very wealthy woman."

As they were making their way to the cave, she wondered if he knew how safe the house would be with leopards in it. Once the kittens grew up, they'd be as big as she was now. Smiling, she thought perhaps she wasn't all that upset about her parents being dead. They'd been treating her as if she were dead for as long as she could remember.

Golden seemed happy to see her. She licked her face and brushed her with her large paws. As Lincoln gathered up the kittens, she helped Golden outside to do her business. It took a great deal out of her, and Morgan had to carry her back into the cave. Once they were all loaded up in the buggy, she sat down with Golden to tell her what had happened.

"So I'm motherless except for you. I know you're a

cat, and I'm only a human, but I think we can get along. When the men start to come — and according to Lincoln, they will — I'll need you to protect me too. I shan't ever marry. Not only that, but I'm also going to make it my life's work to make sure animals such as yourself are as safe as I can make them."

Arriving home well after the sun had settled in the sky again, she made sure the mother and kittens were safe in her parents' big bed. There was a fire in the fireplace for them should the night turn too cold. Morgan also made sure the mother had plenty to eat, having given her one of the steaks her father would treat himself to daily, while she had whatever else he had with his meal.

Sleep didn't take its time capturing her, luring her to a night's rest. It hit her right between the eyes and had her nearly sick with exhaustion. As she closed her eyes, sleeping in her own bed as if nothing had happened, she knew she'd keep her promises to not just Lincoln and the other staff but to herself as well. The animals here would need her, and she was going to make sure they were as safe as they could be while she was still living.

~*~

Four years later

Morgan watched the man as he ran out of her home. How he'd gotten in was beyond her, but now that he was gone with a little less of his fancy clothing, she sat down on the front veranda and waited for the cats to come to her. Over the last month or so, men had been showing up at the oddest times to tell her she must marry them.

They would all come around sooner rather than later. All of her leopards, as well as a plethora of other such creatures, would come to make sure she'd not been harmed or taken away from them. None of the animals would be harmed here, and daily another one or two would come limping into the compound and be welcomed. Golden came to sit at her feet, and she smiled at her when she looked at her.

"He had it coming. We both know that. The pompous ass thought if he could tear at my clothing, I'd allow him to marry me so I'd be happy. He said I'd need someone like him to watch over my money and keep me from dying an old spinster. Apparently, women aren't meant to think beyond having a man around. I'm much happier without him, I think. What did he think I'd been doing here all alone since my parents died? Waiting on someone to rescue me? Not likely." Morgan slid to the floor and put Golden's head on her lap. Running her hand down the length of the cat, she could feel her newest litter wiggling around. "I am worried about you, mistress cat. You're heavier this time with your brood. Not to mention, I know the wound you suffered for me so long ago bothers you more daily. The babes you brought here that night, they have gone on to have their own children. I cannot believe so much time has passed since that night." She thought of something and put her forehead to Golden's. "I just realized you're a grandmother. Congratulations."

"That would make you an aunt in her eyes." Morgan reached for her gun, something she'd been carrying since that night, and found it gone. "You cannot kill me, mistress, but I would prefer that you not harm me either. I have come to speak with you about the good works you are doing here. The one you call Golden, she has asked me to come to speak to you about a great many things. In addition, I have some things I need to ask of you."

"Who are you?" The beautiful woman asked if she could tell her in a moment. "So long as you know that whatever it is you're hawking, I want no part of. We're doing very well here on our own."

"You are doing better than well, I think. The ground is fertile here, thanks to your way of doing things. Not all humans would leave an animal to rot on their land without doing something with it." Morgan told her that other animals took care of it. "They have indeed. Even the things the larger breeds cannot eat or use, the smaller creatures come to salvage what they can. You have a good system here. A system that will not be popular for a great many years."

"I don't want to have to go into town." The woman

nodded, her smile something she thought more than beautiful. "You said you came here because of Golden. She is a cat. How is it possible that she would call to you?"

"Let me start at the beginning, please. The night your parents died, the night you came to help Golden, it was thought that you should have died along with them. Sometimes, with humans, the apple does not fall far from the tree. But you are nothing like them, are you, sweet child? You were not only different from them, but a kinder, gentler person than any of us have ever seen before. We have all been watching you these last years." Morgan asked her who *they* were. "Ah, that brings me to your first question. I am Tellus, the terrestrial being that cares for and is wholly a part of the earth. The earth and the land that you have here. Not from my doing but your own, this land is rich beyond anything man has ever seen before."

Morgan didn't speak, letting all the woman told her to settle into her mind. She'd been alone for most of her life now and had learned not to prattle on when there was no one to talk back to her. Petting Golden, she was glad to hear her purring. The rumbling of her throat was soothing to her for some reason.

"Mother Earth. I've read about you. You're Roman." She said that was correct. "All right. So you're here because I have good land. However, I still don't know why you took time out of your…what I'm sure is a busy day to tell me that."

"You are a jewel among all the stars in the sky, Morgan." Confused at the words and their meaning, Morgan continued to pet her cat. "We, the other earth creatures, have been watching what you were doing here since that night. We've not once had to intervene in helping you care for the animals, all that you protect here. You have lifted a great burden from all of us. Even creatures you may not yet be aware of have found a home here among the others and have been safe from harm. One such creature sits there on your leg. His name is Button."

Morgan looked down at her leg and saw the tiny creature standing there. She put out her free hand, and when he hopped upon it, she brought him closer to her face. Yes, he was a little man, just like the men that had been coming around except for his size. Then while she was watching him closely, he spread out his wings and fluttered above her palm for several seconds before settling down again.

"Faerie." He bowed before her. "I have read of such creatures as this one. They are thought to be a myth. Such as you are, Lady Earth. I have either hit my head, or I'm being visited by creatures as magical as the sun coming up and then resting in the other sky."

"You are seeing magic, my child." Nodding, she laid her hand back on her leg. Button didn't sit on her leg again but stayed on her palm. "He wishes to be with you. To help you in the coming years. For as much as I'd like to say your life will be filled with only riches, we both know it is never that way."

"Nay, it is not. The banker says I owe him great funds for a loan my parents took out before they died. Also, I have a man who is trying his best to catch me unawares, so he might rape me to take my lands. I don't think he means to keep me around much longer than it takes for me to say, 'I do.' They only want what I have." Tellus said she could help her with those things. "Thank you, my lady. But I'm sure you have enough to do now with the earth as large as it is."

"I do. But helping you is not something I take lightly, my child. We, all the creatures in charge of the parts of the earth you now own, are happy to help you. And in doing so, they will get the help they need as well." Morgan asked her what they wanted her to do. "You will do it, will you not? Even not knowing what it is we ask of you."

"I will help the earth for as much as it gives back to us here. And that, as you know, is a great deal. We are self-sufficient here. Water is ours to use as we see fit. There is a roof over our heads when necessary. The fields, as you have pointed out, are rich and give us back so much more than we can eat. I share what I cannot have put up or preserved." Tellus told her she knew that as well. "If you need me to do more, I will do it to the best of my ability."

"Thank you." Tellus looked at her, then at Golden as she continued. "Golden will stay with you until the kittens are born. Her children will be the first of many creatures that will take on this new magic we wish you to help with."

"She's going to die." Tellus nodded but didn't look at her. "I thought when I've seen her around this time, she wouldn't make it for long after. You do know she's the only friend I have besides the people that work here? I've thought about, for long hours, how I will make it without her counsel. Without her snuggling up to me when I need it. I don't know that I want to. But I must, for the others."

"Yes, you will." Tellus told her of the magic that would be given to her. About the babes Golden would have, and how they would go on to be great men, to help her in ways that Tellus and the others hadn't thought of yet. "The magic they will get will help them to be a part of the world of men. To breach such places that even now frighten us a little. We will need you to help them blend into such places. To walk, talk, and act like real men. The abilities we will give them will make them a prize should anyone find out. So it is important they do not give themselves away while men. Do you understand?"

"Yes. I'm to be their teacher." Tellus told her that

she would also be their mother. "I have questions now, but I know I will have so many more when the time comes. I will teach them everything I can. Give them whatever step up they'll need so long as I live. I promise you they will be the best of men. Not like the ones that come here sniffing out an easy way to my home."

"You will not die either, Morgan. You will be around for their children to come into the world, as well as all the shifters that are to be born." Morgan asked her about the men coming around. "They will not come around again should you wish it. Button will have an army of faeries that will come to your aid in that and anything else you might need them for. Do not be fearful of using them either. Rightly so, they are excited to serve one such as yourself. You have been titled with the name Queen of Shifters."

"You don't have to do that, my lady. I said I would help you." Tellus laughed, and it made Morgan smile. "I will do as asked. The rest I will accept as part of my duties, but I don't see myself using it overly much."

"I foresee you using the magic given to you much more than you think you will." Tellus laughed again, bringing yet another smile to Morgan's face. "I will also give you a list of things you will need to invest in. They will fund you better than a bank will, and you will remain self-reliant at the same time. Also, the bank has been taken care of. He will no longer bother you about funds he thinks you owe him."

"Thank you for that." Morgan looked down at her friend and ally in all this. "What will become of me when you no longer have a use for me, my lady?"

"There will always be a use for you, child. A creature such as you will forever bond with the earth and make everything around you a better place. I have such faith in you." Morgan told her she could only do her best. "And that, my child, is all I could ask for."

The two of them talked throughout the morning and into the evening. Ending up in the living room where there was a fire roaring in the hearth, they were served their tea there, as well as juice. She was told she'd need to be drinking a great deal more of the elixir. And that the fresher it was, the better it would be for her after using magic.

At some point, Tellus took her hand into hers and gave her the magic she'd need. The power of it washed over her in waves. So much so that for several minutes she had to sit still in her seat and wait for it to settle out. Not only did she receive the magic, but the knowledge of how to use it. Also, things she'd been told she must invest in. Things that Tellus told her would be worth a great deal in the future.

After Tellus left her to rest, she was told, Morgan sat in the yard at the back of her house. Lincoln came to sit with her a spell, telling her there were faeries in the kitchen now that would make sure the household was safe. Also, he said, he'd been given magic as well.

"It is to keep the house in order. To build out, when you need it, my lady." She said she'd been told she'd need to have a larger house. "I find that hard to believe, but I will do what it takes to have you safe."

"I now have more land as well. Tellus told me there are now five thousand acres here that will be used for the animals in need. No one will be able to enter the land if they wish to harm anything that calls this place home. What am I do to with all this knowledge and wealth, Lincoln? I know I'm to teach the next generation of cats born to Golden, but how much do you think they'll need from me? What am I to do when they go out and have their own leap? I shall be an old woman with only you to keep me company." He asked her if he was immortal as well. "You are. But I was told if at any time you wish to die, I could take it from you. No harm will come to you with it either."

"I think I shall stay with you, my lady. I think we will need each other in the coming years, don't you think?" She said she needed him every day. "You are so kind to me, Morgan, that I wonder at times why your parents wanted you dead."

"They were in love with themselves." She knew that to be true as soon as she said it. Looking at the older man, she smiled at him. "You and I will do the best we can and hope it's right. Someday, I think we'll look back on this and wonder what all the fuss was about. Don't you?"

"I think I will hold my thoughts on that until such time as it comes to an end." He laughed a little. "Do you believe it will come to an end, my lady?"

"No. I don't. I don't have any idea why, but I think we're going to be having something new and strange happening as a daily routine." She stood up when he did. "Let us begin this new phase of our life, Lincoln, and hope we make it work better than the thoughts in my head are making it. All right?"

"Whatever you wish, my lady. We will do well together, I believe."

She hoped so. It seemed like a great deal was depending on her doing just that, making it work for the safety of all involved. She only hoped she knew enough and was strong enough to make it work for all of them.

Chapter 1

Carroll didn't say anything to his mom while she seemed to be killing the dough she was kneading. Something was bothering her. That much was obvious. If he were to ask her about it, he knew just what she'd say. She was good, or she'd work it out on her own. Today it didn't seem to him like either one of her answers was going to work. So, instead of getting her more upset, he spoke about the things he'd come in here to talk to her about.

"There are over six thousand faeries working in the greenhouse today. I'd not thought of it being so close to spring where they'd be needing to put seeds in the dirt. Also, there are a great number of people asking if you're going to be selling the tomato plants you've done for the last ten years. I told them what I tell them every year, yes." No response to him, but the dough wasn't going to be fit to eat if she kept hitting it the way she was. "Also, you might not know this, but Walker's Market isn't going to be selling this year. I think we might have an opportunity to purchase it. He said his children didn't want to—"

"She sent them back." Waiting for more, he didn't have to wait all that long. "Leslie and I took ten bushels of apples to the school yesterday for the kids to have as a treat. The woman in charge of such things, Blanche Mission, sent them back here with a note saying they no longer want our products. How is it possible they can't use fresh fruit and vegetables for the kids?"

"I don't know. Did she happen to tell you why they couldn't use the things we sent to the schools?" Mom told him she'd only said they wouldn't be using them. "I can make a couple of calls and find out. There has to be more to this than just her deciding the kids aren't to get anything fresh to take home."

"I think she doesn't like me." More than likely, that was true. Most women disliked their mom on sight. Her beauty would make even a nun jealous. "I've not done anything different than I usually do around here."

"No. You have a large heart and do what is necessary to get things to the people that need it most." He had a thought since he'd not seen the apples, nor his brothers. "Where did you take the fruit? I'm sure you didn't just dump it in the compost pile."

"Do you have a death wish?" Laughing, he told her he didn't but did get up and push her back from the dough. "Oh my. That will be terribly tough, won't it?"

"No matter. Tell me where the others are and what they're doing with the apples." She told him. "Mom, that is brilliant. And since you're not on the school property while they're being handed out, that makes it all the better. I do hope Ms. Mission sees what they're doing. It will make her all the angrier, I think."

"Angry people make terrible mistakes." He knew that too. "She needs to be stepping down from her position, Carroll. This isn't the first time she's turned away help from this place. If she keeps this up, we'll have to take matters into our own hands again, and I don't want to do that."

"No, you wouldn't. Let me make a few phone calls, and I'll see what's going on." She thanked him as she tossed the dough into the compost pile. "I wanted to get with you today about a couple of things that have come up. And now that I think on it, this might well have something to do with the principal at the school. I got a call from one of our families that works in the federal building. She said someone has complained about how we're not inspected by the government in order to give food to the shelters."

"Since when do you have to be inspected to donate foodstuff?" He said that was on his list to look into as well. "Carroll, what am I to do?"

"I don't understand the question. You mean with this thing? I'll take care of it, Mom. There has to be a reason for her having a burr up her ass." She frowned at him. "That's not what you meant, is it?"

"You don't need me anymore. Every day, I keep thinking someone is going to come along and say, well, you did a great job. The shifters are doing just what we needed you to teach them, and it's time for you to die." He asked her why she'd think such a thing. "I don't know. I've been around for so long now I don't remember even the littlest things about my parents. Not that they were the type to make lasting impressions, but I can't even recall what they might have looked like now."

"Mom, why do you think we don't need you?" She said they were grown men. "We are, thanks wholly to you. We're good men too. None of us have had any trouble blending in because you took it upon yourself to learn everything you could so we'd be able to do what was needed of us. If you think we don't need you now that we're grown men, that's just not right. I find I need you more now that I'm an adult."

"You've been an adult for a lot of years, Carroll. Don't pull that malarkey on me." He laughed. "I feel useless. I work hard—I never haven't gone to work when it was needed. I just feel like if I weren't to show up for something, no one would notice."

Button came into the room, and he shook his head at the little creature. This was something his mom had been thinking about for some time, and he wanted to get to the bottom of why she'd think that way. Button said that he'd talk later and left them to their conversation.

"I would notice. All of us would. I'm betting you see us at least twice a day, if not more. Because we come to you for your advice. Also, your love. No one could have asked for a better mother than you have been for us." She said again that they didn't need her. Pulling her into his arms, he felt her shaking with her pain. Crying, especially tears from his mom, could tear him apart in seconds. "Mom, I don't know where you got the idea that now we're grown men, we have no need for you, but that is simply not true. I think I need you more now than I did as a child. You're my hero. Every decision I make, I ask myself, 'What would my mom think of me if I did it this way?' Or what would you do had you been in the same circumstances."

"You don't have to say that, Carroll." He told her he did if she was feeling like he didn't need her. "I love you guys. And to be honest with you, I do the same thing when I think of an answer for you guys. What would Golden think? Would she allow you to do this or that? She was the very best. I hope you always remember that."

His mom had passed away on their first birthday. They didn't remember her any more than Mom did her parents. She had given birth to them, helped their new mom with them. Then, having been old, she had gone to sleep and didn't wake.

Golden had been buried in the family cemetery that day. No other animal had been put there before or since. But they all knew their biological mother had meant everything to this mom. There were still days, he knew that she would go out to the cemetery not to visit her own parents but to visit Golden and tell her about her day spent with their children.

Where are you? He told his brother Bailey where he was and what was going on. *I thought as much. I just came from the apple handing out thing we started today. There is trouble brewing with the head of the grade school. She's got some heavy things coming down on us soon. She's called in the Food and Drug Administration about the chemicals we're giving to the children when we hand out food. Christ almighty, Carroll, Mom is going to have a fit when she finds out.*

I'll tell her. I think she has it in her head that's what is going on anyway. By the way, make sure you let the rest of them know too. He asked about Mom or the FDA. *Both, I guess. She's feeling kind — What's today? Christ, no wonder. It's Mom's birthday. I completely forgot. Will you figure out something for us to do with her tonight? And we'll also take her to dinner. How stupid are we? Let me know what you figure out for her, and I'll go in with you. We need someone to keep track of this shit.*

They were both laughing when the connection closed. He told Mom about the FDA, as well as what they thought they were doing with the apples. Carroll watched her face. It was amazing to him the way she could hide her emotions as well as any poker player. So when she spoke, he knew this was something she'd been thinking about. The plan she had was just perfect.

"I want you to call Jacob. He has been working in the offices of the FDA since well before this woman was born. See what kind of things they're going to be testing when they get there. Also, if you can narrow down a time, that would be good too. We might as well put out the welcome mat. Since we use no chemicals here, I'm not worried about what they'll find. I just don't want them to harm the trees." He pulled out his phone and made notes on it. "Also, have Marley look deeply into this woman's past. I have a feeling we've crossed paths someplace along the line, and she didn't come out on the upper end of it. Marley has the best luck with searches."

"All right. What do you want to be done with the search? You or the school board. I know two of the shifters from here are a part of the board." She said to make sure to keep them in the loop about what they were doing and the reason why. He wrote this all down. "Mom, I forgot to tell you, two more faeries have been injured in town. I've checked on the places they're working, but there doesn't seem to be anything associated with their jobs."

"Ask Button to see what he can find out. I think he's working with the faeries that came in last night, finding them places to rest up." Carroll knew Button would have more information than they had and decided to seek his help first. "He mentioned to me again that you guys still haven't found yourselves faeries. He said you need to do that before the next season. The faeries are falling all over themselves to be with you guys."

"I'll get with the others, and we'll have a decision by tomorrow. It might be easier just to pick one out of a hat, I think." She said that however they did it, it needed to be done. "I'll get on the others about it too. All right. Anything else you need for me to do? Besides the things to do with the school?"

"There is one other thing." She came around to his side of the table, where she'd been working on making another batch of dough. "I need you to check into some land I've been keeping an eye on. We own just about every bit of the land between us and the town, but there is one patch of land that has never come up for sale. Not only that but the people who used to live there haven't been seen in some time. Like a month, I think I was told."

"Do you think they're gone? If I remember correctly, they were an elderly couple that we helped." She said that was them. "All right. I'll go out there and have a look around. What do you want me to do if I find they're both gone?"

She didn't answer him. Not that he expected her to have an answer to that. It would, he supposed, depend on a great many factors if they were both dead. First and foremost, how did they pass away? After looking over his notes and making sure he knew what he was doing, he kissed his mom on the cheek and left her to her bread.

They really did have everything they needed here on the land. Not only did they have their own water source, but thanks to Mom making sure no chemicals were used on the fields, nothing leaked into the water. There were standing cattle, as well as sheep and pigs, that were used for consumption for them, as well as any of the animals that called this place home. So long as they only took what they needed and left the rest for the next animals, everyone got enough of the slaughter of them to feed their families.

Fruit was abundant year-round, thanks to the faeries. Milk was gathered from the cattle, which made their cheeses as well as anything else dairy. The freezers were all well stocked year-round, and it would be a good thing to have when a winter was especially hard on some of the townspeople. He would bet their family had fed all the townspeople a few times or very close to it.

Carroll found Button just where his mom said he was, in the large field behind their home, helping the injured or exhausted small creatures to set themselves up in whatever they needed. Their land had not only become a sanctuary but also a place to come and relax. He enjoyed watching the little people work the gardens. They could pick a patch of strawberries clean in less than ten minutes.

"My lord. It is a glorious day, is it not?" He told Button he thought so too. "I'm sure your mother spoke to you about your own faeries. I should beg you, but that'll only make you dig your feet in deeper. You're a great deal like her when it comes to that sort of thing. I'm going to pick one for each of you if you—"

"Excellent idea. You know us as well as our own mom. Since you were picked for Mom, it's only fitting that you pick for us." Button blustered. "Come on, buddy. You know we'd take them all if we could. They're so wonderful to be around, and their magic makes ours stronger. If you pick them for us, we'll each have the perfect one for us, and then we'll have one less thing to worry about."

"I can do that. In fact, I have the perfect couple for you right now. They can both get to know you before your mate comes to be with you." He asked why there were two. "Your mate will take the male when she comes along, and you will have the female the way it should be. It will good that you can have a mate that will already understand you. Also, he'll be able to learn your habits and know how to answer your mate's question if she has any."

"Perhaps I shouldn't allow you to pick me one then. That means I'll have a mate." He was only joking, but Button had no sense of humor at best. When you joked about things such as mates and the like, he didn't care for it. "I'm kidding you. Please. Go ahead and find each of us a pair of faeries."

Marking it off his list, he went in search of Marley. Finding him was harder than he'd thought it should have been. Once he told him what he wanted, Carroll asked him to go to the neighboring land. Carroll knew why his mom didn't want to go. She hated death more than she did anything. To her, all things should live forever. But that wasn't to be. They were perhaps a mile from the neighbor's house when he heard back from their guys at the FDA, so they turned around to head back to the house.

~*~

"I don't understand why we're here." Morgan told the young woman, Hanna March, that she didn't either, but they were more than welcome to inspect anything they wished. "You don't sell the things from here, correct? I mean, you could sell them at a stand, but you don't do that either, do you?"

"No. When we have enough for ourselves, we donate what is left over to anyone that wants it. We've been taking fruit for the children at the school for the last few years. They like taking it home to their little brothers and sisters that aren't yet old enough to come to get it themselves." Morgan watched the woman, wondering as she had since she arrived if she had any idea that most of the people she worked with were shifters. "We grow all of our own food here. And meat is still standing until we need it. There are no chemicals to speak of around. We don't even use poison to rid the barn of mice."

Not that a mouse would come within a hundred miles of this place. Snakes wouldn't either, for that matter. There were too many large game animals here that would take them out. Morgan followed her to the orchard. The faeries had been warned not to show themselves, as they had company. She smiled when she thought of Button. Right now, he was sitting on her shoulder like a pin she might have put upon herself this morning.

"This is beautiful. I mean, I've been to a great many orchards before, but this one looks like it was planned out from day one. The lines are all straight. I love the way you've put grapes between the trees so they can hold up the branches. Oh, and look—you have honey too!" She told her if she reminded her, she could take some home with her. "I'm not allowed to take anything with me when I leave a place. But oh, how I would love some to put in my tea in the morning. What flavor do you get, if I might ask?"

"Mostly it's apple, but on occasion, we get a hint of grape too. In the arbors that are beyond here, we have peaches as well as other trees that the bees pollinate for us too." She could have told her they also had bananas, as well as oranges, but since she'd more than likely not believe her, she left it at apples and peaches. "We do sell the honey. There is an inspector that goes through our plant once a year. That's the way we have it set up. I don't want anyone getting sick from that."

"I've read a great deal about this place. I've wanted to come out here since I was a child. You never gave tours of the place, which saddened me greatly. I would have worked here daily had I been able to watch how this was taken care of." She laughed, and Morgan joined her. "My mother, she used to tell me there are a great many animals here that fertilize the lands to the richness that it is. Is that true?"

"It is. Most of them come and go as they please. We don't have anyone killing them for their skins or meat, so they can be safe here. We've had more animals born here than several of the zoos combined. On occasion, we'll go and help one of them out when they have a problem birth. As you can imagine, we have a great deal of experience with that sort of thing." Hanna never once pulled out her kit to test any of the soil or the bark of trees. She didn't take samples of the water that ran between the lines of trees, keeping the roots well-watered. "While here, I can give you a tour of any part of the farm you wish. There is a great deal going on today, but I've cleared my calendar for you. Also, one of my sons will be joining us."

She had no idea where Carroll was. When she'd told him the inspector was here, he told her he was on his way. That had been over an hour ago. When they turned toward the barn where they kept the equipment they used, she saw him coming toward her as his cat. Before she could figure out what his intentions were, he knocked them both to the ground just as a shot was fired over their heads. As soon as the shot was fired, Carroll shifted back to himself and helped her up.

"Are you all right, Mom?" She told him she was, then looked over at Hanna. "I can smell blood. If it's not you, then she's been hurt."

Hanna had hit her head, and she would have a ferocious headache when she woke. But she would be all right. Picking her up, Carroll looked at her for several moments before putting her in the wagon to take her to the house. Since they had no use for gasoline, they'd been using the same buggies they had used for decades.

She was put on the couch in the house as soon as they got there. Carroll put his hand over her head, and it healed the wound. The meaning of what he'd done hit Morgan about the time the girl was coming around. Morgan wanted to ask if this was his mate—one of the sure signs was that only he could heal her—but Hanna was awake.

"Did you see that?" Good at evading questions

she didn't want to answer, she helped the girl sit up on the couch. "That was a leopard. A frigging leopard. He attacked us both. Didn't you see him?"

"No. I didn't see anyone attacking us." She looked at her, then at Carroll. "I think I'll go and make you a cup of tea, Hanna. With honey. I just happen to have some peachy honey from yesterday."

Making her way to the kitchen, Morgan couldn't stop herself from smiling. Even putting her hand over her mouth didn't help. Carroll had a mate. The first of many, she hoped, that would come and take her boys away. Sitting down in the chair, she realized she would indeed do that. Hanna would take her son from her, and soon so would the others. Then she'd be all alone.

Morgan didn't know where her thoughts kept coming from about being alone. It had been in her mind a great deal in the past few months. She would be happy as a lark, then suddenly she'd be so depressed she'd take to her bed. Things today just set in concrete what her heart had been warning her about for some time. She would be of no use to the kings and queens of the land, and they'd take away the magic that kept her alive.

"You could have called to me." She looked at Tellus and asked her if she wished for some tea. "Nay, I wish for you to tell me why you are so depressed about the boys getting mates. I would have thought you'd be thrilled. You'll be a grandma soon, I'm betting."

"They'll leave me." She asked her where she thought they'd be going. "To their own homes. Lands far from here. I won't have them close at hand when I need them."

"I see. And again, why did you not call to ask this of me? Morgan, I think you make trouble for yourself, so I can have a cup of tea with you. Why is it you think we gave you so much land? So it would wither and die when this supposed leaving of you happened? Nay. It's here so your sons can live here, with the land between them and you, and be happy. You don't really think I'd allow them to leave you here, do you?" She told her she didn't know what to think anymore. "Lack of sleep. That's your problem. I have told you I can help you with that. Oh, look, you've made my favorite cookies too. I'm going to have to call David now. He'll be so jealous if I don't tell him you have cookies."

"He has no favorite but eats them all." Tellus told her that was true. Just in case they all showed up, Morgan used her magic to make the tin refill when it was empty. "I don't know what is wrong with me. I feel so out of sorts. Much more of late, too."

"You need to get laid." That startled her so much she choked on her cookie. "I've also been pointing that out to you. Getting laid is a very good relaxant. You need someone in your bed warming your body."

"What a thing to say to me." Tellus shrugged, and

David, King of the Underearth, as well as Joel, appeared in the room. "If you wish to speak like that, I shall never bake you cookies again."

"What did you tell her? That she needs a good man to fuck her? She does." Joel, King of the Trees, got his hand slapped when he reached into the tin. "What? It's true. You'll see a side of the world you've not seen before with a little sex. Or a lot. I think you need a great deal, Morgan. You have been celibate for a long time."

"I will have you know that I've been working for the lot of you. Fat lot of good it does me. You've made fun of me at every turn. Why, I ask you?" They all three told her it was because they loved her. "Be that as it may, I am not going to justify anything you say about my bed partners or the lack of them. Why are you three here? Don't you have work to do?"

"We do. It's why we're here." They finished off the cookies three times before they got down to business. "Morgan, what if we were to tell you that we believe you have been too helpful for us."

"I'd say that is no fault of my own. How can I be too helpful? Unless it's making it so you don't have as much to do on your end. If that's the case, then I'm happy I could help. All of you, all the kings and queens, have so much to do that I don't know how you get half of it finished." The three of them looked at each other. "What is it? What are you trying so very hard not to tell me? Spill it. You know how much I hate it when you give it to me in bits and pieces."

"We've heard how depressed you are." She said she'd been depressed for some time now, and no one had bothered. "Perhaps, but we've figured out a way for you to have some fun. You do remember what fun is, don't you, Morgan?"

"I don't like any of you today." She sat there watching the three of them refilling their glasses with juice. Filling the tin up with things other than cookies, then dismissing it. Button came in to sit on the edge of her plate. Morgan looked at him. "I take it you've gotten all the boys faeries."

"I have, my lady." He laughed. It was a giggle that sounded like bells one might have found on a small tree. "They're all ready to go now, and I have to tell you, it was a great deal more fun for me after they told me to pick them. I do know them as well as you do."

"You do. All right. Since you have done such a wonderful job, Button, you might as well sneak into the living room and see how Carroll is doing with his mate." Button nearly fell off the plate. "And before I forget, could you please find out who shot at us today? There was some confusion afterwards, and I simply forgot about the fact we were targets."

It occurred to her that she was the only one talking. Looking at her three dear friends, she asked them what she'd missed. They asked her about the shooting. Just as she was going to blow it off, as she usually did when she had this sort of trouble, Carroll and Hanna joined them in the kitchen.

"I was making you tea." Getting up, she moved around the kitchen in a way that Hanna couldn't see what she was doing. The tea was made in record time, thanks to the magic, and she sat it before the young woman as the cookie tin was put there as well. "These three are friends of the family."

She only ever introduced them as friends. If they wanted to share more, then that was up to them. So when they told Hanna who they really were, she wasn't the least bit surprised to see that Hanna knew a bit more about shifters than most did. But she was still going to have a great deal to learn about these shifters.

Chapter 2

Carroll let his brothers do most of the talking. They were shy at first but soon got over that when Hanna asked them what they did for a living. The answer usually centered around whatever job they were doing at the moment, but this time they told her some of the things they'd done over the years. Carroll had a feeling, however, that Hanna was just humoring them. She was still coming to terms with some of the things he'd told her in the living room.

"You're an ancient." He nodded and said they all were. "Okay. I guess. I don't know why you'd tell me something like that when you don't look a day over your late twenties. But I guess we'll get to that too, right?"

"We could get to it sooner if you would believe me." She shook her head. "All right. Let me tell you about the leopard you saw. That was me."

"Okay. It was you." He growled at her. "Look, Buster. I've been around for a while now. And I know for a fact that there are shifters. However, I don't for a second believe you're as old as you're implying, nor do I think you've been living here with your five brothers and your mom when she doesn't look a day older than I am. Not to mention, you told me your family works for the kings and queens of the earth. What on earth do you take me for? A fruit cake? I'm not. I'm not stupid either."

"No, you're far from stupid. What can I do to convince you that I'm just what I said I am?" She told him to hush for a moment. He watched her face as she looked around the room they were in. "My mom used to weave when we were younger. She made just about all the rugs in this house at some point. Also, after a while, she started to weave some heavier rugs to be put in the pens of the animals when they were giving birth."

"That bow and arrow. It's very old. Are you going to tell me that was yours too?" He said it was his mother's. That she would use it when they were younger to teach them how to run down prey, wounding the animals with the arrow just enough the cats could figure out what they were to do to be in the wild. "That sounds cruel."

"No. We would eventually capture the animal and eat it. Mom has a very good ecosystem going on here. We don't bury the dead, but allow it to go back to the earth after all the other creatures around here get whatever they want from it." Hanna stared at him. "I'm very old, Hanna. So are the rest of us. We, my brothers and I, were the very first shifters ever made. Mom—Morgan—kept us safe after our biological mother passed away on our first birthday. She's been our everything for a very long time."

"You told me you're my mate." He nodded. "I know what that means. And unlike most of the people I talk to, I don't have it in my head that you're going to order me about and make me do things I have no desire to do."

"My mom wouldn't allow that to happen either. What is between us is a partnership. There will be times when you need me more than I do you, but I also know I'll need you a great deal more than anything I've encountered before. That would include breathing and my heart beating." He could tell she didn't believe him. It was all he could do not to laugh at the skepticism on her face. "Would you like for me to shift?"

"No. I do not want you to shift." Carroll couldn't help it. He did laugh then. "You're very confusing. First, you tell me you're my mate. Not that I'm yours, but that you belong to me. Okay. Good. Then you tell me you're very old. That's fine, I guess, but harder for me to swallow. You have a lot of knowledge about things that only comes with age. I can almost believe the first shifter thing about you and your brothers being the first shifters. However, believing that would make me have to believe that you're very old, as you said. That's the sticker, I guess. You being old. Not just old, but ancient."

"My mom has some company in the kitchen. They're older even than we are. Sort of our honorary aunts and uncles, I guess you could say." Carroll stood up and put out his hand. "If you come with me, I can help you to understand a little more about our kind. Also, we'll see what you have in the way of magic."

"Magic?" He nodded and took her hand into his before she could pull it back. "What sort of magic? I mean, am I going to be able to turn you into something small and harmless, then step on you?"

"Why would you want to do that?" She just glared at him. "I've given you no reason to want to squash me. However, if you really must, let me introduce you to my family first. That way, they can rescue me from your booted foot. Also, you should know that you're an immortal."

Hanna stagger-stepped twice before they made it to the kitchen. Once when he told her she was immortal, the second time when he told her who was in the kitchen with his mom. He was, however, impressed with how well she'd taken who they were. And not once did she tell them she didn't believe they were who they thought they were. Of course, it might have helped his cause if they were to have proven it to her. But all in all, he thought this was a good deal more fun. Now they were all seated in the living room, with his brothers telling Hanna some of the things they'd done over the years.

"I must tell you all something while you're here." They all quieted down, and he looked at his mom, who had been unusually quiet. Tellus stood up and looked around the room. "I remember the day you were brought into this world, all of you so small yet the healthiest of babes ever born. Then, when your mother passed away, leaving the world a much sadder place with her absence, I thought my heart would break."

"She was a leopard queen, Golden was." Joel blew his nose and smiled at Bailey as he continued. "You have her coloring when you're a cat, my boy. Even your eyes are the same beautiful shade."

"Mom was never a shifter. She knew when she had us that we'd be the first. However, she wished not to remain living. Her body, she told us, was too worn down. Too beaten up from being in the wild for most of her life. Plus, there was the bullet wound that bothered her more the older she got." Hanna asked him how she was shot living there. "She didn't always live here. Morgan was just a child when she was taken to the woods to be murdered. The men that had been hired to kill her for her parents were killed by Golden. She took a hit that night."

"You have lived a very adventurous life, Morgan." Mom nodded and told Hanna she didn't know the half of it. "So you guys are really old. And you're magical as well."

"We are. I don't shift, not that I didn't want to. But I did have the greatest job ever in being asked to raise these six." Mom smiled at them all. "They are, in order of birth, Carroll, who, as you know, is your mate. Then there is Leslie, Bailey, Marley, Scout, and Shiloh. All were born on the same day within hours of each other. I was asked to help them in the world of humans so they could blend in without any kind of hiccups that would put them in danger."

"You did a good job of it too, my dear. And that brings me to what I have to tell you. Your mom is going to go away for a while. We've decided she needs to see the other worlds, the ones she and the rest of you have helped over the years." Carroll looked at his mom as she sat there. "She really does want to go but is afraid that leaving you guys behind will somehow scar you for life."

"I did not say that. I said I wanted to go, and that was it. I didn't say a word about actually packing my bags and leaving." Carroll asked her why she wasn't going. "I've never been anywhere and don't feel like I missed something. Why do they think I need to be away now? I don't get it."

"You need it, however." It was Shiloh that spoke up this time. "I've noticed you're tired all the time now. All of us have. You don't rest. I know we don't sleep anymore, but you must rest sometimes."

Carroll spoke softly to Hanna. "When we were created, they decided we didn't need to sleep. That living with magic, it would be unnecessary for us to need to shut down. That was a mistake they fixed in the next shifter group. We don't need to sleep, but we must rest sometime during the day, even if it's only to sit in the living room and watch a little television. Or read a good book. Which is what we usually do." Hanna asked him if he enjoyed reading the classics. "I do. We have a lot of first editions around here that are signed. And while I know you're going to find it hard to believe, they were signed just for us."

She only looked at him before turning back to his mom. Carroll knew he was having way too much fun with her not believing him. But he was also enjoying having her around. Even in the last few hours that she'd been here, he realized how much he'd missed teasing someone. Having fun at their expense. Carroll wouldn't take it too far, but he was enjoying her anger as well.

"You need to go, Mom. If for no other reason than you deserve it." She asked Scout if he was trying to get rid of her. "Never that. Not ever. You are my heart, and I would perish without you. But since we were born, you've never done a single thing for yourself. And as you said, I think you'd really enjoy seeing the other worlds. I know it's been a dream of mine to see the water king, as well as the creatures no one else has seen."

It was still in debate while they had their dinner if Mom would go or not. The others had left—they had realms to run—but they did leave behind a magical book for Hanna. She was to read it or not, but Joel said it would give her a better understanding of not just what they were but some of the magic she had gotten from Carroll. It took Hanna about an hour to realize she had already gotten some of the magic from them finding one another.

"This is just too much." He said he could understand that, and he would answer anything she had a question about. "And if you don't know the answer? Will you go to the others and find out? I mean, you already know the mother of all things. And let's not forget the king of the trees. Who else might you inquire with for answers to my questions if you don't know the answer?"

"Are you upset that I know the other realms' rulers or that I might not know the answer to your question?" When she made her way out onto the deck at the back of their home, he looked at his mom. "I don't know what I've done."

"She is confused, Carroll. As anyone would be, that has been thrown into this situation. Just let her think and do not interrupt her with answers that she might well have no need for at the moment." He asked her if she meant him telling her that he was old. "Yes. What did that have to do with anything between the two of you?

Nothing right now. Just ease her into this as you would a newborn that needs to know a great deal of information. But they have plenty of time to get around to learning it. She'll come around. But in smaller doses than you've been giving it to her."

He went out onto the deck and sat on the steps that led out to the yard. He saw Sunny coming toward him and put out his hand. When Leo joined him, he asked Hanna if she wanted to meet his faeries.

"Faeries? I suppose you'd have those too. All right. But no funny stuff. I'm about to have my mind — Oh, look at him! He's so handsome." Carroll was sure that Leo was going to bust his buttons off his vest when Hanna said that to him. He flew to her outstretched hand and bowed before her. "Leo is a good strong name, did you know that? It means lion. I bet you have the heart of a lion too."

"Thank you, mistress. I am pleased to serve you." Hanna looked at him, but when he opened his mouth to explain, she stopped him by putting her hand up. "You will need a faerie in the coming years, my lady. Sunny will be with Lord Carroll here, and we will work together to keep the two of you out of harm's way."

"Will I be in harm's way? Or will Carroll be in harm's way when I have to strangle him?" Leo looked at him, his eyes wide with shock. Carroll told Hanna that they took everything someone said to them literally. "I'm not really going to strangle him. I'm sorry about that. But in the last few hours, it's been tempting."

"Lord Carroll is the being that helped me be a part of this household. When I was just born, he came to the fields and found me lying upon the dirt. I would have been a brownie had he not found me and turned me over to the faerie queen. Not that I have anything against the other creatures, but I didn't want to work in the human world as a big person. Brownies can do that, you see." Hanna nodded and smiled at him when he winked at her. "Sunny is a bit older than I am, so she had magic I didn't have. When we were chosen to be the faeries for the two of you, we were able to share what we had so we'd be better at protecting you. Also, we have gotten more magic too. It's wonderful to be able to serve you in any way you wish, my lady."

"I'm overwhelmed at the moment, so don't tell me much right now. I'm still dealing with all the things that were told to me earlier." This time she glared at him. "I'm sure Carroll meant well, but I feel like my head will—" Carroll shook his head so she'd not say what was sure to upset Leo. "My head will have too much in it right at the moment. If I have questions, or it's something that I need to know right now, then you can tell me. But for the moment, let me deal with the knowledge that I know now."

They sat out on the deck for hours. Mostly it was

Hanna speaking to the faeries, but she would occasionally ask him something. He was about as comfortable as he'd ever been sitting out there and was glad she'd not wanted to go into the house.

"I have a job." He nodded and told her he had one as well. "I don't know that I want to continue working. I mean, I could, I suppose, but I'm not sure I ever enjoyed my job all that much. But here, I would love to learn all there is to know about this place. It's like its own little world that outsiders aren't allowed to intrude in."

"That's about right. We do have outsiders come here. We have cattle that we use for both milk and meat. We used to make all the cheese for this area, and Mom realized that if we were only to make the cheese and other dairies we needed for ourselves, it would provide jobs for others if a plant were to open up for the rest of the town to work in." Hanna told him that was brilliant. "You will be surprised, I think, to know what other things we have going on here that make us self-reliant. You'll notice that there are no cars or any kind of gas-powered equipment here. Not that we couldn't go into town and buy gas, but the pollutants would harm the other creatures that call this place home."

"The faeries." He told her there were all manner of animals here that people thought were myths. "Like? And please don't tell me too many right now. I'm beginning to settle in my head."

"In addition to the faeries that live here, there are also brownies, trolls, and gnomes." She asked if they were around where she could meet one of the gnomes. He nodded to the garden at the bottom of the stairs. "They're here now?"

"The gnomes live in the house gardens year-round. You'll see that no matter the weather, it is always warm in the herb gardens, as well as the flower beds. That's to shelter them from any kind of cold or heat. In return for us giving them a place to live, they give us fresh herbs as well as medicinal things that need to be used on some of the other animals that live here." She asked him about the trolls. She thought them to be mean. "They are if they are treated badly. The ones here have in some way been hurt. Whether it be from physical or emotional pain, they come here to rest and heal. Not all are welcome here. If they have caused trouble elsewhere, they are only given one chance to stay here without causing trouble. We've only had to ban two from ever coming back."

Carroll could tell by the look on her face the moment one of the elders came out of his little hut. Mr. Weeds and his family had been living here since before he was born. When Hanna sat down beside him on the steps, he made room for Mr. Weeds if he wanted to share the seat with them.

"Mr. Weeds, I'd like for you to meet my mate, Hanna March. Hanna, this is the patriarch of the gnomes around here, Mr. Thaddeus Weeds. He's in charge of all the gnomes around the world. However, he has chosen this place to call his home." Hanna put out her finger to the elderly gentleman, and he looked up at him. "She's new to this land, sir. If she offends you in any way, 'tis my fault."

"I'm sorry. Did I do something wrong?" She took her hand back so quickly it even startled him. Mr. Weeds took his long pipe out of his mouth and told Hanna to put her hand back for him. When she did so, instead of taking it, he opened her hand and sat down on her palm. For as long as he lived, he'd never seen him do such a thing before. "You're very handsome, aren't you?"

"I am at that." He looked over at Carroll. "You've got a right beautiful mate here, Carroll. Right beautiful indeed. If you've not a mind about it, I'd like to take her to meet some of the other people that live here. I know you'd like to do it, but I can hear that brother of yours cursing like he's got himself a potty mouth."

"I'll see to him if Hanna doesn't mind." She smiled at him, and Carroll could have easily given her his heart right from his chest for it. "Mr. Weeds, if you'd not mind, can you take a little of your precious time and help her with the rules as well? I don't want her to be hurt because I've been lax in making sure she knew what to do in the presence of so many otherworldly creatures."

"Aye. Yes, I can do that." Carroll kissed her on

the cheek and stood up. "You'd be better served, young Carroll if you were to take this little lady to dinner tonight. Show her off to the queen and such."

"We have a great deal to talk about before I think of taking her to see the queen. She's met Tellus. Joel and David were around earlier as well." Mr. Weeds nodded as he held onto Hanna's fingers as she stood up. "If you need me, Hanna — not that I think you will — but all you need to do is think of me, and I'll come to you."

"All right."

Hanna and the gnome were talking as they headed to the woods. She'd not be any safer with Carroll than she was with Mr. Weeds. He was far and away the most respected and feared creature he knew.

Carroll found Marley in the barn at the back of the cottage his mom had asked them to check out yesterday. He had no idea what he was doing, but he waited quietly for him to stop talking to himself, or for that matter, to someone that Carroll hadn't seen yet. When his brother looked up, he could see the marks on his face. It looked as if he'd tangled with another cat.

"No. Nothing like that. But I do have to return to the cottage on the other side of our land. There were a lot of raccoons in the place when I got out here. I don't know who was more startled, them or me. They were only protecting their young." He asked him if he'd been in the house yet. "Not as yet. But I can smell death. I didn't want to take the chance of going in without the police. I've called for them to aid me."

Almost as if he'd conjured them, two cruisers pulled into the driveway. Shaking hands, Carroll was a little thrown when he could feel not just their emotional turmoil, but he could also feel that Officer Daniel Penick was ill. It took him a bit longer to realize the man had terminal heart disease.

"What's the matter with you?" He looked around, then at Marley. "You've been standing there staring into space for the last five minutes. Are you going to go into the house with us or not? Get your head on, will you?"

"Yes. Of course." They went to the front door of the house and knocked. Both the men with them were human. Carroll was sure, however, that they could smell the decomposing corpse as well as he did. As soon as the door was opened, all four of them took a step back. The smell was horrendous. "I can go in for you and open some windows. In fact, why are they closed up?"

"I was thinking that too. Whatever happened here, had you not been doing a wellness check, it might well have been a good deal longer with them closed up like this. If you'd not mind, Carroll, we'd surely appreciate it if you were to open the windows a bit. Also, I don't need to remind you not to touch anything."

"I promise I won't." Carroll moved into the house and to the window in the living room. Nothing in there, but the smell was getting stronger as he made his way to the back of the house. The kitchen was where he found both of the bodies, and it looked like murder. Not touching anything in the room, including the window that was closed up tight, he made his way out to the cops. "They've both been shot. Head wounds. Mister is sitting at the table. Wife is on the floor. The fridge is open, but everything in it is bad like it has been a few more days than we thought."

Letting his family know what was going on, he waited with the police to see if they needed anything from him or Marley. The couple had been ambushed, it looked like. The missus had been shot in the head—the mister as well, but while someone was in front of him. He wondered why anyone would want to harm this old couple. They didn't even go into town much, so he didn't think they'd have much in the way of enemies.

"Your mom told us someone shot at her today." He'd forgotten about that and told Officer Penick that was right. "Do you think you can find the bullet? I know it's a long shot, but I thought we'd test it against the ones here. If I remember correctly, this house sits right about in line with your orchard, correct?"

He had to think on it, but he thought the man was right. The back yard proved to have a line of sight view of not just the orchard but about the same place he'd found his mom and Hanna. Carroll returned to the house to explain what had happened.

"I was in the yard for some work, and I heard the first shot. I knew my mom was showing the FDA personnel around, so I went to make sure she was all right. The second shot nearly got them both. I didn't even think about it again after making sure that Mom and Hanna were all right." He told him that was when he found that Hanna was his mate. "I should have called you then. I'm sorry."

"No worries. I don't think these people were killed that day. Coroner will have a better timeline for us on when they passed. This is just a guess, but I'm thinking they were killed because whoever shot at your family would have wanted them out of the way." That was just where his mind was going now. "I don't suppose you have any enemies, do you? I don't know who it would be. You guys are the rock of this area."

"We do now." Daniel looked at him, wide-eyed. "One of the personnel at the elementary school. Ms. Blanche Mission. She's been complaining about the fruit and things we give to the school. That's the reason the FDA was here in the first place. She told them we were giving away contaminated foods and that we've never been certified."

"I'm not sure, but I don't think you have to be certified by them if you're only giving the stuff away. You in no way make a profit from it, correct?" Carroll told him they didn't. "I'll have to look into that one for you. I'm not sure. But if you have yourself a Fed here, then she'd know. I'll look into this woman for you. She must have a burr up her butt about something with you guys."

"Officer Penick, can I help you?" The man looked around, then back at him. Obviously, he didn't want anyone else to know. "It wouldn't be any trouble for me to do this. I like you, and I know you have a young family."

When he turned away, Carroll let him. The emotional turmoil was stronger now, and he didn't have to touch him to feel it. Turning back, he asked him what the long-term effects would be if he were to do this. And what he would want in return.

"In return? Nothing. I told you, I like you, and I don't want you to have to suffer needlessly. You need to be around for your little ones, and that would be good for all of you. As for side effects? You will live a great deal longer than you would by not having me help you. You might even get a little extra. It's something I can't predict until I heal you. The disease is taking hold, and it's covering up anything else that might be there." He asked if he could think about it, talk it over with his wife. Carroll handed him his cell phone, one he rarely used. "You don't have a great deal of time left. Call her and tell her."

Daniel came to find him a little while later. His wife must have busted his chops over wanting to ask her about it because the man was giddy with happiness. Apparently, his wife was all for him being healed.

Putting out his hand, Carroll waited for Daniel to put his hand into his. He hoped he wasn't having second thoughts about this. If he did, Carroll was going to call his wife himself and tell her.

"I will owe you for the rest of my life for this." Carroll told him as long as he was happy and well, that was payment enough. "No. I will owe you."

Putting his hand onto his, he felt the surge of power run from his hand to Daniel's. Putting his other hand atop Daniel's, he saw everything the man had been suffering with. Also, how he had planned to kill himself as soon as tomorrow. When he sat down in the grassy yard, Carroll joined him there.

"Christ, that was amazing." They both laughed. "Seriously, I don't remember feeling this good in all my life. If you could bottle that, I'm sure a lot of people would be beating a path to your door for some of it."

"That is precisely the reason we don't tell anyone." Daniel said he wouldn't tell anyone. "I know you won't. I knew that before I made the offer. You're going to be fine. The little extra you got is that you're going to heal a good deal faster than you did before. That doesn't mean you won't die from a head or heart shot, but you'll be able to heal faster."

"Thank you. Thank you so very much."

Daniel walked back to the house and finished up the crime scene. Carroll just sat there, thinking about nothing much, when he saw movement out of the corner of his eye.

Not making the person aware of him seeing her, he reached out to figure out not only who it was but also why they were here. It was Blanche. She had indeed murdered the older couple here, but she thought she'd have a lot more time before the house was checked.

Carroll dug deeper into her mind to find out her motive for trying to kill his mom. The reason was astounding. He'd have to get with his mom and tell her right away. While he had no idea how to get the message to the police, he knew his mom was going to have to be extra careful from now on. The woman was going to hurt his mom because she was opening a greenhouse in town, and she hated that Mom was competition.

Chapter 3

Hanna sat on the large rock and watched as the little faeries worked. She wouldn't have seen them, she was sure, but for Mr. Weeds pointing them out. It wasn't that she didn't want to see them, he told her, but she wasn't using her magic to do so. Hanna was going to have to get used to this stuff before she missed a lot of other stuff.

"Mistress?" She smiled at Leo and asked him if he could just call her Hanna. "No. Oh no. I cannot do that. I would be too familiar, and the others would be jealous. But the reason I've come to you now when you are resting is that the faeries here need some help."

"Whatever it is, if it's within my powers, they'll have whatever they need." Leo smiled at her. "You already knew I'd do it, didn't you?"

"I did. You have a kind heart. They need for some

of the trees to be dropped." She looked at where they were and could see the sun streaming through the trees. "They can only plant the seeds that are good in shade. This area in another hour will be in darkness. The plants they want to use are in need of the extra sun. I have spoken to the trees, and they'll help, but you need to ask Lord Joel if you might be able to help the little ones."

"How do I talk to him? I mean, do I just call someone and make an appointment?" He laughed, and she smiled. She didn't want to tell him she'd been serious with her question. "How do I contact any of the others, for that matter? I'm thinking that felling trees wouldn't just affect the planting area, but also the earth, as well as any creatures that might be using them as shelter."

"That is an excellent thought. Yes, indeed. Excellent." Hanna had noticed that when he was thinking, his wings fluttered so quickly it was difficult to watch without being ill. The colors on it were lovely but too bright with the sun shining on them. "I will contact all that will have some involvement in this. Yes, you were the right person for this job. I will return directly."

She had no idea how long that would be but settled on the rock to wait for just a little while. Hanna had decided last night that she wasn't going to work for the federal government anymore. Making an impact on the earth wasn't done by sitting behind a desk for most of her workday but going out and doing something about it. Working here and living here would give her all the work she wanted to do and fulfill her lifelong dream of touring this little slice of heaven.

"Hello." She turned to see who had spoken. "Don't be alarmed. Leo told me to meet him here when I could, and this was as good a time as ever. My name is Holly. I am in charge of the landscape of this realm."

"Do you know who else is coming?" Holly told her that both Joel and David were joining them, as well as the mother herself. Mother Nature. "She must be terribly busy. I didn't mean for her to be taken from her work. Any of you, for that matter. It was only a thought that I needed to clear things before I got a crew out here messing things up."

"You did very well. Leo is quite pleased with the way you thought of us. I have no trouble with the shoring of the trees, but then the permission on which to fell would have to come from Joel." She told him what the faeries needed and what she thought might help them. "That's an excellent idea. What will become of the fallen trees?"

"I would imagine, like the rest of the things that fall to the earth, they'll be left where they lay. I'm not sure, now that I think about it if I can make this sort of decision." He told her she was the only one that could. "What about Morgan? I mean, this is her land. Right?"

"It is all of your land, but yes, Morgan owned it

before even we came here to help. However, she will tell you that if you see a need, you are to take care of it. Here she comes as well. This will be a good meeting, I think."

Chairs appeared around the rock she was on, and a cushion materialized under her. She smiled at Leo when he asked her if she was comfortable.

The meeting was wonderful. Morgan did tell her she was glad to know Hanna was going to be helping out when she saw the need and that if she thought it was a good idea, Morgan would as well. The kings and queens all agreed that felling the trees would be helpful in so many ways other than just sunlight, but it would help the other undergrowth that was struggling to take hold as well.

There wasn't any need for a crew, she soon found out. Joel simply moved along the trees, touching the ones that would be taken down. When he asked for everyone to stand back, the trees simply appeared on the ground as if they'd been cut. The sun coming through the nice opening had all the little creatures clapping and singing. She even joined in on some of the celebrations.

The faeries didn't waste too much time in their happiness. Getting to work, they were planting seeds at a high pace. She had to look away a few times, the speed making her slightly ill, but she was so happy she could take part in this.

"I would like to ask you a favor, Hanna." She

told Morgan she'd do anything for her. "Don't say that. I might want you to do something terrible, and where would you be? No, the boys have been staying at the house since they were born. As they got older, they arranged their rooms to be like a home. I believe Carrol has five bedrooms in his part of the house. The others have a few, but not as many. My favor. Could you go and have a look at what could be your home? I know you've been staying at the hotel in town, but that seems silly when we have so much room here. If, after seeing the home, you don't care for it, then you can build. But, and this is me being Mom, could you please live close enough that I can see the two of you once in a while? That sounded terrible, didn't it?"

"Not at all. I'd like to make sure I can come and see you when I want. You're a wonderful person, and I love spending time with you." Morgan thanked her. "I'll go and have a look at it when I'm finished here. Mr. Weeds is showing me around today. Carroll went to help his brother Marley."

"They're at the cottage. The couple that lived there was found dead this morning. Murdered. Carroll knows who did it and why, but he can't figure out a way to tell the police without telling them how he found it out." Hanna said she might be able to help with that. "You could? That would be wonderful. The culprit is Blanche Mission. She wants me dead so her open market will do better. I know that sounds nuts, but people have hurt me for far less."

"I heard about your parents, Morgan. I'm so very sorry about that. But you did come out on top." She smiled at her, and Hanna was happy she'd brought it up. "I'll go over there later and see what I can do by having a look around. It might just be as obvious as her leaving fingerprints. However, I'll have a look around and make sure they know my suspicions. I was an agent before I took on the duties of the food and drug part of the job."

"I'm so glad that you and Carroll are mates. I think with your knowledge of the laws and your wanting to work with us, it's going to go a long way in making sure things are done legally. I've never had to deal with this sort of thing before. But the more people know about us, the more they want a piece of it. Not necessarily in a good way, either." The two of them ended up on the far end of the property by just talking and walking. The place they were at now looked like it had been there forever.

"Mostly, it was built by my grandparents. The winery hasn't been kept up since Carroll and his brothers came into their own. It's not that we didn't want to do it, but there always seemed to be one more thing that needed us more. I was hoping someday it would be running again, with a label on it from here. Do you know what the land here is called and why?"

"Morgan's Leap. I know what it means, but not

why it's called that. I mean, other than the obvious." Morgan laughed and explained to her more about her parents. "So you changed the name of the place from White Plantation because they used slave labor to pick the grapes and never paid their people. They don't sound like people I would have liked to have known. I know that you pay your people now. They seem to be making a good living here as well."

"Yes. I also gave up the name White, and me and the boys became the Golden family. Mostly all we have here working are the creatures from the earth. Occasionally a human will come along for some reason and stay here. Lincoln was part of the staff when my parents were alive. He's been there for me every step of the way. Then about ten years ago, he decided he wanted to be out of doors and out of the house, and he moved to one of the homes that was built for him." She asked her what it was he did now. "You're going to think this is funny, but he hangs out in the nursery. There are babies born all the time, and he said it makes him feel so much younger when he gets to be around the newborns. They're mostly trolls or an occasional brownie that might find their mate who has children, but there are usually one or two born daily."

"Okay, another place I have to visit." They were laughing again. It felt so wonderful to have a female friend after working in a male dominated workplace. They didn't treat her badly, but she never was going to be one of the boys. Here she felt free and needed. She told Morgan that. "I do need to ask you why you're taking this vacation. Is it because I'm here? I'd hate to think I've run you off."

"No. Never that. But I'm exhausted. I've not been taking care of myself since I took this on. I wanted to be the best, something as a child I never obtained. Not being the best, but having someone recognize what I'd done. Sounds vain, but it's not. I worked very hard to make sure the animals that worked here were in good shape. I was never allowed to go see to the darkies, as my parents called them. I would get them beaten, and myself too, if I tried. So I stayed focused on the animals. Then that branched out, much like you did with the trees today. Finding things that would make their lives better, like cutting down a few trees. When the animals worked better, the people here did as well. Not that my parents ever noticed it, but I did, and I made that an adjustment to seek people out that did something great as soon as I took over this place." Hanna told her how much she was enjoying watching the way things were working here. "It's taken a very long time to get it right. Sometimes we still don't have it correct, but we get closer all the time. We're still having issues with the irrigation for the gardens, but it's a lot better than it was."

"I saw what you're doing with the plants that need a great deal of water. I don't think I would have thought of putting in spigots along the rows so you could water them to their hearts' content. Shiloh said you had traded meat for the things needed to make it work. That's wonderful."

Morgan said they used the barter system whenever they could.

It was a lovely afternoon. She not only knew more about what was going to be her home, but she enjoyed spending the day with Morgan. Hanna thought she looked better, more rested. She certainly didn't seem as stressed. Making a mental note to seek out her new mother-in-law daily just for walks like this, the two of them ended up on the back end of the house. It was, Morgan told her, where the boys lived.

"You do know they're not boys, right?" Hanna said they were forever her little boys. "Okay, but I'm just going to point out to you that they're bigger than you are and more than likely still afraid of you. I can see it in their eyes when you gather them around you."

"Good. That's what a mother should do to her kids. Scare them a little." Hanna loved how the entrance to each of the sections of the house was different than the others. She could tell which one was Carroll's without being told. "He so loved when he did glass cutting. I think for a while there, he was making a good living at it."

"I didn't realize they all had jobs outside of

here until last night. Why didn't they just stay here to work?" Morgan told her she didn't want to make them do anything they might not enjoy. The projects here were hers. And since the boys had decided they liked it better here, they worked on their own projects. It usually ended up with the same goal in mind. Make the world a better place. "Bailey still teaches classes at the vocational school. He told me he likes seeing the kids' faces when something they've planted or put together grows into something sustainable."

"He is creating the next generation of people like us. Or so he tells me. Every year they have a garden put in. Some of the kids around here might be getting their only fresh vegetables from it that year. But once they are finished, there is a contest to see who has the best. After that, they have a cookout, then trade the things they've grown with others in the same area. It's worked out so well that we bring some of the kids here a couple of times a year to sell off some of the produce we raise, including pumpkins. A few years ago, we cleared a lot of pine and let them sell them for Christmas trees. It has not only given the kids a great way to make money but also the town helps out as best they can."

Carroll joined them as they were sitting around the pool. She was getting used to him kissing her when he left or found her. She was sure he wanted more from her, but at the moment, she was still getting used to being around him. Not to mention just being around his family.

"I was just telling her that you've got a nice place here. You should show her around, Carroll. Oh, you're the first that I'm going to tell. I've decided not to go on the little vacation. I have found that since Hanna so willingly puts up with me, I'll stay until she runs me off. You've got a good mate here, son." Morgan left them then, going into the house, whistling a tune she'd never heard before. "Dinner in town tonight, Carroll. Since the lot of you forgot my birthday."

"Shit." Hanna laughed. "We had plans to take her out last night but got sidetracked with all this other stuff going on. Do you want to go too? I hope so."

"Yes. I'd love that. Now, show me your home. Your mom seems to think I'm going to love it. I hope so. I really love being this close to your family. Whoever had this idea about living here all together gets my vote for a nice gift." He opened the door to his home, and she stood looking inside. "I don't know what I expected, but this—Carroll, this is what I have been dreaming about in a home all my life. And I've only seen the entrance."

~*~

Carroll had been living in his part of the house since he'd been an adult. He was seeing things he'd not noticed before, like how there were cobwebs in the corners of his living room. Dust in the corners. His windows were less than pristine.

"I'm so sorry about this." She asked him what he was talking about. "I should have thought you'd be coming here and had someone go over it with a dust mop or something. I didn't see the dirt until just now."

"It's not dirty, Carroll, but a little mussy. It's fine." She sat down on one of the two couches that were in the living area. When she stood up, he looked to see what had made her hop up so quickly. "Okay, that has to go. That spring or whatever it is will hurt someone."

He showed her around the rest of the main floor. The kitchen wasn't in much better shape than the living room, but at least he'd done his dishes this morning. There were, however, a couple of things he should have done, and one of those was to water his herbs. The other was he should have taken out the trash. When she told him how much she loved to cook, he felt even worse by how badly the place needed updating.

"Will you please just chill out? I'm sure that had you known you were going to have trouble that would have required the FDA to come in and inspect things when a woman tried to kill off your mom, you would have been able to update things. You didn't, so we'll work on it when we do. I'm not at all unhappy with the way this looks. Yes, it's outdated, but in a way that makes me think of past times when you were growing up." Running her hand over the wide countertops, she smiled at him. "My grandma had counters like these. I think they were the same color too. She would make the best cookies in the world when I came over."

"My mom is famous for her cookies. I'm not sure which ones—the others have their favorites that she bakes when she knows they're coming over. How did you talk her into staying?" She told him she didn't. "She seemed a lot less stressed. I noticed that as soon as I came up on the two of you. And I've not heard her whistle in ages. You must be good for both of us."

"Did someone notice something different about you?" He said Marley had remarked on how he was forever thinking. "You didn't think before? That doesn't sound like you."

"I've been getting lost in thought, I guess you could say. I'm thinking too hard on what-ifs. I've always been the one that would see things through the eyes of a criminal or something like that." She asked him if he'd been a cop in one of his jobs. "No. An attorney. I think we've all tried our hat at that particular job. The only one that stuck with it is Leslie."

"He is the family attorney, I'm to understand." Carroll nodded and followed her to the pantry and decided he needed to hire one of the brownies to come and fix up his kitchen with staples and such. "Do you guys all get together to have a meal together? I mean, like a night a week that you don't plan anything else but having dinner with your family?"

"Wednesdays. Mom usually does the cooking, but here lately, she's been having one of the faeries do it. I think that has a lot to do with her being stressed too. Not getting to cook. Not that she couldn't, but she's been really pushing herself to the limit lately." She said she noticed that. When he moved into the dining room, the next room by the kitchen, he realized he was alone. Going back through the little open place, he found her standing in front of the window where the sink was. "Anything wrong?"

"No. I don't think so. I do, however, believe I've seen my first troll." He came up behind Hanna and put his hands on her shoulders. Pointing to the left of the monstrous troll, he showed her that there were smaller ones out as well. "They're not really what I'd consider cute and cuddly looking, are they?"

"Not particularly, no. Mom told us that it's a face only a mother could love. I believe her. The trolls have only been around here for the last decade or so. They have their children deep in caves where no one will bother them. Their gestation period is about a year long. And when they're born, the offspring are helpless to the point of nearly dying before they can get to feed from their mother. It's not a nursing thing, but gross. She regurgitates whatever she ate last and feeds it to them." She looked at him, horrified. "I know. The first time I saw it, I couldn't eat for a week. I'm not going to tell you what she had eaten, but it took me a long time to get back to having it for a meal. I still get the willies sometimes."

"I wouldn't eat ever again." The two of them stood at the window for another few minutes. It was twilight now, and some of the creatures that didn't care for the daylight would start coming out. She also got to see some of the wild pigs that roamed the lands, as well as some moose. They were here simply because his mom had such a joy in seeing them. "Their babies look just like the adult version, except for the horns."

"Again, a face only a mother could love." They did make it to the dining room. He'd never gotten around to putting anything in here except a few boxes that were filled with dishes and such. "I rarely eat here unless I'm in the kitchen. Then it's usually standing up at the counter. I don't think any of us have a dining room set up but Mom."

"I have a few things that were my parents' and grandparents'. Would you mind if I brought them here?" He told her he'd be happy with anything she wanted to bring here. "Your mom thinks I should be staying here. Not paying the hotel bill. Would you be here with me, Carroll?"

"Yes. In whatever capacity you'd like for me to be. I'm sure you've come to realize it's a large home. I have plenty of space if you'd rather take the master bedroom as your own." She asked him how it worked with him not sleeping. "You won't have to either, but we do need to rest at least once a day. Also, I don't know if Mr. Weeds told you this or not, but you do need to eat a great deal of fresh fruits and vegetables every day. More when you're using magic."

She took a step towards him. Then another. "I've been thinking about a lot of things since I figured out who you are to me. One of them is that I really like you. I don't know that I love you yet, but you're beginning to grow on me." He thanked her. "You're very welcome. I want to work on this place with you. Not alongside you all the time, but I'd like to be here to help. I'd also like to help your mom with some of her projects. Take some of the load off her. Can we have children?"

He had to think how to make his mouth work for a few moments to answer her, but she seemed to understand. There wasn't much space between the two of them now, and he was finding it difficult to think much less function.

"I don't know." He said he'd check on that for her. "I think we can. I'm almost sure of it, but I'm finding it difficult to think at the moment. Are you going to kiss me, Hanna? It's something I've thought of all day." She smiled at him. "You're very beautiful, but when you smile, you light up a part of me that I didn't know was inside of my heart."

"That was the perfect thing to say to me." He

leaned toward her, taking his time in the event she wasn't ready for him as yet. "I want to get to know you sexually, Carroll. I want to feel you touching me too."

"You're saying the right things to me too, Hanna. Before I get too far gone and don't remember my name, will you marry me? As soon as possible? I'd like to be able to tell the world that I'm the luckiest man on the planet." She told him she could do that. "Good. The sooner, the better. Do you have a family to invite?"

"Nope. Just me." He nodded his mouth just a hair's breadth from her lips. "Kiss me, Carroll, then take me to bed, please. I want to get to know you in all senses of the word."

Picking her up in his arms, he realized he should have kissed her first. But then he also knew that had he done that, they'd never have made it up the stairs. As it was, he was really working hard at not laying her down on the carpeted steps and having his way with her.

The room was just the way he'd left it. Messy. Not bothering with telling her he needed to straighten it up, he used his magic and made the room look like something he'd seen in her head. That made him realize if nothing else did, that they were alike in their ways of having a home look. Old versus new won out with her every time. He couldn't wait to show her the other rooms in the house, but that would have to wait. Today he was going to mate and bond with her, and that was all he could think about.

"You're much too slow at this." He made them both naked. "Oh, much better. If you can do this all the time, there is hope for us yet. Take me, Carroll, before I explode right here and now."

"I aim to please, my dear." Dropping her on the bed, he laughed when she bounced twice. "I have fallen in love with you, Hanna, and cannot wait to make you mine."

Chapter 4

Hanna looked at the man poised over her. He was tall, handsome, and fit. There wasn't an ounce of fat on him, she'd bet. And it would have nothing to do with how many times he'd been to the gym or how much weight he could lift on the barbells. No, it was simply that he was fit because he worked hard on the things he enjoyed. One of them would not be what he saw when he looked in a mirror either.

Sitting up, so she was sitting on the side of the bed, she looked up at him. "I've never been with someone like you. I don't mean a shifter, but a man who cares. You do care about me, don't you?" Carroll told her how much he loved her. "I believe, despite what I said before, that I love you. I think I have for a very long time. Though it sounds stupid, I think I've been in love with someone like you all my life. I'm so glad you found me."

She touched her fingers to his chest where his heart was. It was beating strong, and she stood to put her ear to it. Smiling, she told him it was beating a little faster than before. Looking at him when he pulled her chin up so she could, Hanna knew that there would never be another person in her life that she loved more than this man.

"You're naked." She looked down at herself and acted shocked. "This is how you're going to be, aren't you? Silly at the most intimate times? Not that I care. I don't think there is enough laughter in the world as it is now."

"I agree." She got down on her knees and kissed the leaky tip of his cock. "There should be much more of this too."

Taking him into her mouth, she moaned when the taste of him slid across her tongue. When he told her to do that again, confused at first, she looked up at him and nearly swallowed him whole. His face was a mask of need, his mouth pulled tightly over his teeth like he was straining hard to keep from screaming. Reaching up with her right hand, Hanna cupped his heavy balls in her palm and was rewarded with him coming hard enough to make her glad she was able to catch each drop of his release.

"Christ, again." She didn't give him room to change his mind but swallowed him past the thick muscles in her throat. It was like having a hard rod there, but she'd not pull away for all the money in the world. Then he started fucking her mouth.

It was wonderful to have him there. The sounds he made had her sliding her fingers down her body to have her own release. As soon as her fingers fluttered over her clit, she screamed out around his cock so hard that she was dizzy from it.

Suddenly she found herself on the bed, Carroll at the bottom. Saying not a single word, he buried his face in her pussy and bit down gently on her clit. Coming again, harder than the first time, she gripped the spread on the bed hard enough that her fingers ached with it.

Over and over, he'd bring her to the edge and drop her. She was sure that every last one of them was going to kill her. If not, she'd be nothing but a puddle of her body that could no longer move. When he started up her body, kissing and nipping at her skin as he made his way to her breasts, she got a renewed strength that she'd never have dreamed of.

"You're mine." She nodded. "No. Say it. Tell me you belong to me and no one else. Say it to me, Hanna."

"I'm yours, and you're mine. I will never belong to anyone but you. You have my heart, my soul, and my everything. Take me, Carroll. Please? I need you."

She screamed when he entered her. It didn't hurt so much as it filled her. When she moved, her body adjusting to his, she cried out again, coming over and over as her body accepted his.

Breathing hard, she kissed his cheek and tasted his sweat. Looking at Carroll, she pulled him to her and kissed him again. She could taste herself on his lips. The creaminess of her was there for her to see as well.

He made love to her slowly then, his body in time with her as he filled her. Hanna had never been so conscious of a man before. Never felt the grooves and lines of a man's cock. His fingers, touching her, seemed to leave her with the feeling of being shocked, like in some way he was filling her with magic. When he threw back his head, roaring as only a large cat could, she watched as the two of them, him and his other self, came hard enough to have her blinking out several times as stars, rainbows, and unicorns danced behind her eyelids.

She woke to him lying atop her. Hanna wrapped her arms around Carroll, feeling so much love for him that she ached to show him. When his soft snore touched off a giggle in her, she was glad he rolled to his back, taking her with him. She laid there for several more minutes before she slid off his warm body to the side of the bed. Looking at the great grandfather clock in the room, she was amazed that not only had several hours passed, but it was now nine in the evening.

Her protesting body told her she needed to take a long bath. However, a few things buzzing in her mind had her taking a quick shower then dressing in some light clothing. Pausing outside their bedroom, she wondered if Carroll realized he did sleep and left him to it. A rested, well-sated man was a wonderful man.

She left the bedroom and ended up in the kitchen. Making herself a light snack, she took her sandwich out to the back deck and froze when she saw what was out there. Hanna wasn't sure if she should run or stay still, so she opted for sitting down on her butt and calling to Leo.

"She won't hurt you, my lady." She asked him if he was sure. "I am as sure as it's going to rain tomorrow. She's a unicorn. Not very many of them left around anymore. The only pair are the ones here. They're to have themselves a little one if I don't miss my bet. Goodness, the queen will be so happy to know that, she will."

"Why is she here? I mean, it would seem sort of dangerous for her to be out in the open like this. Don't you think?" He said she was the safest she could be by being here. "I have to admit to you, Leo. I've always wanted to see one. They're much more beautiful than they're portrayed in the cartoons, aren't they?"

"Oh, I don't know about that. But all unicorns are pure white. It's so they can blend into their surroundings so well." She didn't understand that until Leo whistled and the unicorn simply disappeared. "See. Being no color at all, she can take on the ones around her easily. The only true color on her is the horn she has. It's pure gold and diamonds. That way, if she needs to protect her or her young, she knows it won't be broken while doing so. The male, he's over there, see him?"

She did, and he was so white her eyes watered from the purity of the color. The hair, she supposed it would be called that, around his hooves was as long as hers was, flowing gently around his feet like a carpet he was stepping on. But it was his mane that had her wanting to touch it. It was woven in interlocking braids that lined along his back as if he'd only just come from a hairdresser. When he came toward her, she held her breath.

"If you sit still, he'll allow you to touch him. He knows you're my mate." She reached up and interlocked her fingers with Carroll's as he spoke behind her. "Once he's close enough to us for you to reach out, make sure you bow before him, for he is the king of all unicorns. Even though they're the last of their kind, he will forever be the king."

"She's going to have a babe, Leo said." Carroll looked at the female as she came towards them. "She's so beautiful. I would very much like to touch her belly. I don't know why, but I have a need to do so."

"Then you must, my lady." She went to her knees when the male was close enough. Reaching up her hand, she bowed her head and waited for him to touch her. When the sharp point of his horn stuck her, she didn't jerk away but left her hand just where it was. "He's asking his lordship if he might taste your blood. He is telling him it was his intention to cut you, but he knows now he should have asked."

Apparently, Carroll gave the male permission because, in seconds, his wet tongue licked away the blood. She was nudged once. Leo asked her to stand up and look at her treat. There before her was not only the male but his beautiful mate as well.

"May I touch her?" The male nodded, his hair blowing in the slight breeze as he did so. "I'll never harm her, sir. I will lay down my life to protect you both."

Putting her hand on the female's back, she ran it down along her spine to her swollen belly. There she felt the babe move under her fingers. Flattening her hand over the movements, Hanna knew something that perhaps none of the others knew. Looking at only the male, she smiled at him.

"You're to have twins. A boy and a girl. They're healthy and doing well. If you'd like, for some reason, I have the exact date and time they'll be birthed too." He nodded again, and she told him everything she knew, including that the female would be born first. "You're so lucky, my lord. Twins, from what is in my head, are a rarity for unicorns. I'm so very happy I was able to share this news with you."

She felt so wonderful that she wanted to tell the

world what she knew. However, she knew if word ever got out that there were really unicorns and that they were on this property, they'd be dead before the next sunrise. Petting the two of them, having fun when they pranced around the yard, she asked Carroll if they really flew.

"They do, but not here. They have to be extremely careful not to be seen." She said she understood that. Just as she was going to go to Carroll, who was sitting on the deck with Leo, he laughed. "Turn around, Hanna. You're seeing a side of them that few will ever know."

The male was standing up on his hind legs. Wings as pure as the rest of him were spread out behind him. She knew they'd be as soft as down, and they'd be strong too. She bowed before him again when he did the same to her. A feather fell from his wings, she noticed, and instead of leaving it where it was, he picked it up with his teeth and handed it to her.

"If you take that, you'll be blessed. I can't tell you what he will bless you with, but I know you'll not ever have to worry about returning the favor he gives to you. Nor will you ever be alone when you are in need of help." She asked Carroll if he had been gifted a feather. "No. I don't know anyone that has been but you. My mom, even taking care of them for as long as she has, doesn't have a feather. Take it, Hanna. It will be a great disservice to him if you turn it down."

She took it. The power of it surged over her in

wave after wave. When he bowed again, she held onto him as she did the same. Staggering a little, she sat down on the ground to watch the couple move around the yard as if they had not a care in the world. It occurred to her that she could understand what they were saying. When she realized that, the female, Mag, came to sit beside her.

"If you put the feather into your hair, it will be there for all to see. It will show that you have the power of our kind behind you." She asked the beautiful Mag what kind of power would she need to show. "There are many that would seek to harm you simply because you are a mate to a very powerful leopard. Not only is Carroll the oldest of his kind, but he is the being that humans will want to emulate. If they cannot do that, some will seek to destroy him. Since you are his mate, they will attack you first. With the feather in your hair, all will see that you've been chosen to be protected by the unicorn. A group of beings that can kill humans as easily as with just a look."

"But there are only the two of you." Mag laughed and told her to look toward the woods. When she did, Hanna saw nothing at first. Then as things started to come into focus, she saw so many she couldn't count them all. "No one knows. I can understand that, but even Carroll thinks you two are the only ones."

"It is the way it should have been until he met you. He will, with you at his side, protect us. And in turn, we'll protect all that he is as well." After getting instructions on just how she was to wear the feather in her hair, she slid it up from behind her ear to the top of her head. "You are now marked as a protected one of the unicorn."

The sun was rising when the family and the others went back into the woods. Carroll and Leo had joined her on the lawn, and it was Leo that pointed out she had a white streak in her hair. The feather, so she wouldn't lose it, had become a part of her hair. She thought it so amazing that she'd not only been the first chosen to see the unicorns but was to be a part of them as well.

"You'll have a lot of other creatures wanting to mark you soon." She asked Carroll why they'd want to. "Mostly from jealously. I've learned that creatures of the earth are much vainer than humans if you can believe that. But now that you're my mate, they'll want to make sure you, of all the people in the world, are protected. Because you're the first mate to the very first shifter ever created."

"I guess I never thought of the power that would wield." He told her that as she got older and met more of the creatures here, the more powerful she'd get too. Nodding, she watched the sun coming up behind the trees. The way it seemed to warm the earth in degrees made her think of something else Mag had said to her. "I can understand the animals here. All animals, she told me. That will come in handy, Mag told me, once you and

I start caring for the ones that need us most."

"I was going to talk to you about that. Mom said she'd like to be able to hand off some of the things she's been doing now that you're willing to help her. Are you up for it?" She told him she thought she was. "Good. We can start tomorrow. Or I guess today. There is going to be a meeting at noon that we'll have to attend."

Whatever the meeting was about, there were a lot of notes she needed to go over beforehand. After going over a few of them, she realized it wasn't so much a meeting as it was a sort of court to make sure the rules were followed, as well as enforcing them on those that didn't follow. She might like this job, she thought and was glad to have something to do. At least she thought it would be fun. Laughing to herself, she picked up the second file of paperwork and settled into it at the table to work.

~*~

Blanche didn't know who had tipped the police off about the old people, but she was pissed off about it. Now she'd have to figure out another place where she could see the Morgan Leap. She thought it was the most ridiculous name for a farm she'd ever heard.

"What do they do there? Leap around like a bunch of frogs? Stupid people."

Blanche wasn't sure why she hated Morgan so much. She didn't know her. She had only seen her from a distance the few times she'd tried to off the woman. Her sons were always around town, doing this or that for the downtrodden. Which, to her estimation, was about everyone in the little town.

The knock at her front door startled her, and she went to see who she was going to have to yell at. She didn't want anyone around her while she was plotting. Opening the door, she was temporarily dumbfounded by the beauty that stood there. Then she smiled, and it was like a part of her heart was filled with something more than meanness, which she took pride in having.

"Ms. Mission? My name is Hanna March. I'm with the Food and Drug Administration. I'm here to talk to you about the complaint you filed with—"

"I didn't give my name when I called." She realized she'd just admitted to calling, and that pissed her off more. "How the hell did you find me?"

"We're the federal government, Ms. Mission. We know everyone." She supposed that was true. They were forever nibbing in everyone's business. "I'm here about your complaint. I need to ask you a few more questions."

"I suppose you might as well come in then. But don't get comfortable. I have things to do today." The woman said she just needed a few questions answered. "Well, I'm not going to serve you tea or some shit like that. You'll ask, then get out."

The woman sat at the table in the kitchen and

pulled out her notepad. "What is it that made you suspect the food being given in the Leap donations were contaminated?" She said they were just too pretty. "I'm sorry? I don't understand."

"The apples were perfect. Like the ones they use chemicals on to make them have no bugs and shit in them. You know, spraying them down with all kinds of things that a kid doesn't need in their bodies. Not that they don't get enough of that shit now, but that's what made me think they were filled with chemicals. Did you check them out?" She told her they had. "I'm betting they're using something that hasn't even been heard of before. Tell me what you've found, and I'll laugh my ass off with you."

"Nothing. I've been out there before coming here. The tests we did on the fruit still hanging on the trees show no chemicals at all in or on them. They aren't using commercial fertilizer, but manure that they get from their own animals." Blanche told her that wasn't right. "But it is. I've made you a copy of the test reports that came back. In fact, some of the people in my office want to go out there and see how they can have their own orchards work as well as they have at Morgan's."

"They're just giving them away. That's not right. How will a person be able to compete with them if they're just giving shit away?" Hanna told her. "So when they give out fruit to the kids to take home, they're making the same donation to the grocery store as well. Well, ain't she just about the dumbest person around. That has got to cost them a lot of money. And for what? Fame? That doesn't surprise me either. Stupid woman."

"I wouldn't think she's stupid so much as a nice person trying her best to help out her community." Blanche snorted, and Hanna smiled at her. "Anyway, I wanted to make sure you knew what was going on with the investigation and what our findings are." She looked down at her notes, then smiled bigger at her. "One more question. Did you have a reason for wanting her to fail? You mentioned competing with her, and I was wondering what sort of plans you had that would have anything to do with the Morgan's Leap."

"Well, I am thinking about it." She asked her what she would sell. "Fruit. I have my own trees in the backyard here. Also, I'm dabbling in some herbs. I think she has them too, that she gives away willy nilly."

"I'd love to see it." Hanna stood up as if she'd invited her out to inspect her own orchard. "If you'd not like to go, you can just point me in the right direction, and I'll have a look on my own."

"I'll go." She didn't want her to see what she had in the back of her place. But for some reason, the need to show her was making her ill. When they were in the backyard, it was all she could do not to stand in front of her trees and tell her to go away. "My herbs are just over here."

To call what she had an orchard was well overstating it. There were two trees, neither of them looking like anything but dead branches someone put dirt around. Her herb garden wasn't any better. When she'd purchased the herbs with the intention of planting herself a kitchen garden, she'd gotten bored with it and abandoned the entire area. It was also more work than she'd thought it would be. Blanche had thought that you just plopped them into the ground, and that was it. But there were ones that needed lots of sun, some that needed no sun. She also had a couple of them that said they spread. Into what, she had no idea. Now there were dead and dying herbs still in containers on the ground.

"It's not really that much, is it? I don't want to sound rude here, but I don't think you would have been able to compete with her at all with the little bit you have here, Ms. Mission." She told her that she was only getting started. "I see. Well, I'm going to have to see what sort of chemicals you're using. It would only be fair since you were accusing her of using chemicals."

There was no time at all to stop her. The woman plucked two of the nastiest apples she'd grown off the tree, took a scoopful of dirt from the ground around them, and then cut into one of the branches. Not so much a branch as a switch. Standing there while she put everything in bags, she'd asked Blanche to sign off that she'd gotten them from her trees.

"This doesn't seem right somehow." But instead of telling her, she didn't want to sign off, Blanche found herself again doing something she didn't want to do. "I didn't call you here to do this for my things. They're the ones messing up and feeding the kids shit that is going to give them more brain damage."

"As I have told you, there are no chemicals in their land or in the fruit. If we find something in your orchard — well, I mean trees — we'll have to make sure you've cleaned it up before you can sell them. I don't mean commercial chemicals like are made for this sort of growing, but other things that might be in the soil." She asked her what that could be. "For one thing, it could be drain off from someplace else. Or even that you're putting something in the ground that would damage young minds. I'm going to turn this in on my way back through town, and you should hear the results very soon."

Blanche found herself standing alone in her backyard, watering her nearly dead herbs. It had never been her intention of doing any such thing, and she wondered if that woman had put some kind of hex on her. Tossing the hose to the ground, she screamed when it twisted up, spraying her several times in the face and body while she tried to catch it. Damn, but things were not going well for her today.

Going into the house, she found that Hanna had left her not only a business card but a list of chemicals that would not be accepted if found in the soil test. There was also a list of fines she might incur if she were to find them. Looking at the list, a very long one at that, she knew they were going to find a lot of them in her yard. She'd been dumping whatever she could lay her hands on to make her trees produce like they were supposed to.

Sitting at the kitchen table again, Blanche wondered what she could do now. She wanted to win. It didn't matter what the winning would be, but she wanted to make sure Morgan didn't win at all. She didn't even want her in the stratosphere. There had to be some way she could kill off the woman, gain her grounds, and then make the kind of money she wanted to.

A small voice sounded someplace near her ear, and Blanche turned to see who it was. The bug or whatever it was stood up. She noticed that not only did the thing have a face, but feet too. Cocking her head a little, she wondered what sort of spell she'd really been hexed with and started to flick the little thing away.

"I'll hurt you if you harm me." She stared at it, her hand poised to do just what she was thinking. "I'm not allowed to hurt you unless you try and harm me. But you flick at me. There will be hell to pay."

"From you? A bug? I'm not at all worried about what you'll do to me." She laughed a little, knowing the sucker couldn't do anything to her. "You're no bigger than the shit I took this morning, so I'm not worried in the least bit about you."

She would swear to anyone that would listen—and few did when she started talking about the little bug—that it had beaten the shit out of her that morning. Not only did it knock her around the room a few times, but it had given her not just a black eye but also her sprained wrist. But people didn't believe her, and some were calling her crazy behind her back. The little creature told her what people were saying about her too. They all thought she was a nasty person for taking up a cause against their beloved Morgan.

Blanche had tried blaming it on Morgan when she went to the doctor that morning. But that didn't go over well, so she revised her story to say she'd gotten stung by a bunch of bees, and it had given her some kind of hallucinogenic infection.

"You have learned a good lesson, haven't you?" She told the little bug he'd better watch his back. "It isn't possible to watch one's own back. But I'm not worried about you anymore, Blanche. I have had a little taste of your blood, and I know you're as mean-spirited as I thought you to be."

"I am not. I'm a good person." She thought he had told her, several times, that his name was not Bug but Fly, but she didn't want to name it. It made it more real that he was there, she thought. "I've never actually harmed anyone in my life."

"Do you not count killing someone as harming them? Or attempting to kill someone as harming them? You have killed two people that *bothered* you, and you murdered them where they stood. Like the Hendersons. Whatever that means in your tiny heart." She asked him who they were. "The older couple that did nothing more to you than live on the property next to Lady Morgan's. Also, you have put an attempt on Lady Morgan's life several times over the last years. Shame on you for lying to me." She huffed at him. "That sounds like a noise a hippo would make. Are you now pretending to be one of those? Because it would be an easier thing to believe than you being a good person."

She didn't know why, but she thought it had called her a hippo. Deciding to let him have this one dig today, she set out for the store again. There had to be a reason someplace that Morgan was forever giving shit away. And the grocery store, she'd figured out, was the best place to get gossip. Or to spread it. Whatever worked, she supposed.

Going to the store to pick up some things she could have for dinner, she was met by the manager standing in the doorway, telling her she wasn't welcome there. Not ever again. When she asked him what he was talking about, he told her that anyone who badmouthed the hand that helped them was not welcome in his store.

"So you're telling me you don't want my business? I spend a lot of money in here." He said he looked it up, and in the last month, she'd spent ten dollars and demanded half of that back when she told him the peas were not what she wanted. "They weren't what I wanted. I told you they were too small. I like fat peas when I have to eat them."

"They were called petite peas. I think the name alone would have cleared that up for you. The fact that you bought four bags of them and returned them goes to show what sort of person you are. Demanding something for nothing. No, I don't want you in here again. I've made all my employees aware of you as well. Do you know what they did when I told them you were no longer allowed in my store? They danced around like it was a good thing. You're a mean-spirited person."

The Bug laughed all the way back to her home. She didn't have any more luck shutting him up than she had trying to get around the store manager. Blanche was going to have to do something drastic about this. She couldn't have people keeping her from food. Then she wondered if there was a law about that. She'd have to look it up when she got on her computer.

Chapter 5

Looking over the notes for their first meeting, Carroll was glad his mom had come along with them. She said she'd tell them what she could about each person and point out some of the laws they'd broken.

"They all have excuses for what they've done. Some of the things they're here for are silly things that no one will get up in arms about. Like this one. Caster is being accused of stealing water from the creek running by his neighbor's home. It's not a crime that I see, but Flower doesn't want him in his yard. He smashes his pretty flowers. Since he won't accuse him of crushing the flowers, as that is a bigger crime that his neighbor would be in trouble for, he says he steals." Hanna asked her what she did about that. "I just suggest that Caster gets water from the area set up for anyone to gather water and send them on their way. Usually, that's all there is to deal with. But today, you have a larger issue. The dragon flowers that have been planted by the lady earth have been coming up missing. The thing is, they're very popular with the florists around town and beyond. Someone, I think, is stealing them, but I don't know who it is. That is a very bad issue. Flowers that grow here are for the animals, not the humans."

They sat there with their mom for an hour before she said she'd return. Mom was still handing off projects to each of them, and he was glad for it. Even Hanna said she thought Mom looked more rested in the last few days, as well as happier. Her whistling had become something everyone was looking forward to hearing.

After this hearing, there was the one for the flowers. After looking around, knowing what he did about the flowers, Carroll knew who was taking them. However, the reason why was something he wanted to know as well. He looked at Hanna when the people for her trial stood up.

"My lord and lady, I have come here today to ask that you expel Margie from being here any longer. I don't like her." Hanna asked the little faerie, Brown, why he'd want someone expelled. She thought the area was large enough for everyone. "'Tis, my lady. 'Tis. But Margie is not telling me, yes, and I need for her to be my mate."

"I see. Does your kind take mates as the other creatures hereabout do?" He said they didn't breed, so no, they needed no mates. "Then I don't understand why she needs to be your mate. What reason could you have to force me to make her your mate? Or toss her from here to make you happy? I'm going to need a better answer than just that she won't tell you yes."

"She has such a lovely place, my lady. It hangs out over the waterway. There are even some windows she's put in. A nice place. Even the flowers on the tree seem to grow just for her." Hanna told him it was nice to have a lovely home. "Exactly. I have a tiny home. I have no windows to speak of. I don't want to have to find the glass that would fit. I will admit I am very lazy, but I do work hard when I must. Also, my home has no view like Margie's does. It's just looking out over the back end of the tree, and I have no shade in the fall. She needs to be mine so I can live in her home too."

"You don't love her." He said he liked her all right when she was nice to him. Which he told them wasn't all that often. "So, in a plot to make her take you into her home, which I'm assuming you'd not help with the upkeep of, you'd have me toss her away."

"It is her home, my lady. I'd not expect her to clean up my home if we were to be living there. That would be just silly when we both know her home is much nicer anyway." Hanna looked at Carroll, then back at Brown. "If you have to expel her, that will work out fine for me as well. Then I will simply move into her home and call it my own. That way, everyone is happy."

"Except for Margie." He said she'd have to give up something if she wasn't going to cooperate with him. "How about we do this? You will simply live in your home or find yourself a new one. If you do that, then someone can go into your home and make improvements to it so they'd have a place to live."

"No, no. That won't work. Do you have any idea how much work goes into building a home for yourself? More than I want to work with. No, my way is better. Don't you see? She'd be able to have another home, and I'd not have to put up with living with her. It's a win-win for everyone."

I would expel him at this point. But, if you would be so kind as to tell Hanna to not say it until the very end of her sentencing, he'd have to do it as it was told to him. Does that make sense? He told his mom it did and then asked her why she'd not told Hanna. *I don't want her to think I'm stepping on her toes. She is doing so much better than I would have done with that man. I would have squashed him years ago had I had my way.*

While laughing, he told Hanna what his mom suggested. When she smiled at him, he sort of felt sorry for the faerie. Margie was asked to stand, and Hanna asked her why she didn't want to be living with Brown.

"Not that I blame you at this point. He does seem to have a very high opinion of himself." Margie agreed, telling Hanna that she knew his plan and didn't want any part of it. "Just for the record, Margie, you have no desire to have Brown as your mate? And you do not wish him to have anything to do with your home?"

"No, my lady. He is a pain in the backside, and I'd just as soon be expelled than to have to put up with him for the rest of my days." They all looked at Brown when he huffed. He was picking his nose like he wasn't the center of attention. "As you can see, my lady, no one—I doubt even his own mother—would want him nearby."

"All right. I've made my decision." Brown actually moved toward Margie, putting his arm around her as if he knew what the outcome was going to be. Her punching him in the belly knocked the little man back, but he didn't move back to his own seat. "Brown, you will build yourself a home you can live in. With a view or not. I don't care. You will be kind to others—no more assuming that they'll just do what you want all the time. Also, and this one tickles me to no end. You are hereby expelled from the land known as Morgan's Leap."

The little man simply disappeared. Not only that, but Morgan told Carroll when he asked her about it, so did his home and his belongings. Brown would no longer be a welcome faerie, nor would anyone help him with his tasks. He would be a branded faerie for the rest of his days.

No one said a word for several seconds. Then as

if a large pall had been lifted from the area, all the little creatures, and large ones as well, clapped and celebrated. It seemed to him that Brown would never be missed, nor would his ways. Carroll was glad that, first of all, Hanna got to expel him, and second, that she was here to see how well her verdict was received.

"The next case involves the dragon flowers that are grown on this land. They are a special plant that not only feeds the dragons when they come to visit from the other realms but are also the only known medicine to cure some diseases that are death to all trolls. The flowers have been spotted in several nurseries hereabout, as well as in arrangements that have been delivered to homes. We are here to take to task the person or persons that have been taking them." The faerie and the brownie he knew had taken them stepped forward. To have so readily told on themselves made him think there was more to this than just someone trying to hurt their lands. "What do you have to say for yourself?"

"We had no choice, my lord." They peeked at him, then lowered their heads again. "The woman in town, she told us that if we didn't do this thing for her, she would pluck our wings off us and all of our family. First, we were only to bring her a single seed. The human said it wouldn't be enough. I told her we could not do that. So she killed my mate and—" The faerie, he thought his name was Pix, fell to the ground in apparent agony. "She killed my mate, your lordship. Because when I told this woman there would be no more, she said I'd do what she said, or all would die at her hand."

"Do you know her name? This murderer. Do you know what she goes by?" Carroll could see they were terrified. Of him or the woman, he wasn't sure. "You know how to handle these flowers so that you're not covered in their dye. There is only one reason that you would be stained as you are. Did you not use magic to handle them, so I'd see the blood-red stain on your hands?"

"Yes, my lord. We talked it over, and Mary and I decided it would be better to have your wrath come down on us than to betray our families and others around here to the woman luring them to their certain death." Pix looked up at him. "We don't know her name. No, but we do know where she is. I don't know how she was able to get us. I am still confused about how we were lured there in the first place. I am so sorry, my lord."

That would take some looking into. Whoever this woman was, if she was the one trying to kill his mother, she'd be gone soon enough. But they needed proof for his mother to take action against her. Killing one of the faeries was akin to killing off the most endangered species there had ever been. Their magic disappearing when they were killed would have a rippling effect for decades to come. Asking the two of them, Mary and Pix, to come to him, he looked over their hands as well as the cuts on their bodies. Asking them if she'd done this as well, Mary answered this time.

"We are both willing to die for what we have done. I have told my mate should I not return, she isn't to mourn me, but to know I was killed because I did a very big wrong to all of us." He glanced at Hanna when she put out her hand. Mary stepped up on her palm like she was going to be executed. "I would thank you, my lady, to make it quick and to not make my mate suffer. She knew nothing about this until I told her today."

"I have no intentions of killing either of you." She looked at him, and he nodded. "This is a terrible thing that was done. I don't mean the dragon seeds but to you and your families. To think that someone out there has harmed you has my blood boiling in anger. Tell us what she looks like, then we'll take care of this for you. It is only fitting that you be a part of this murderer's downfall."

As it turned out, it wasn't Blanche but someone related to her. It was her sister-in-law, and they lived in the same house. Something had to be done about the two women, and Hanna wanted to confront them both now. But it was his mom that would mete out the punishment, and he and his brothers would be right there with her when she did.

The rest of the trials were small things that took no time at all to take care of. Someone was complaining about how the brownies in one section of the land were taking too long of breaks. However, since they came in a full two hours before the others did, Hanna let them have the extra break for doing some of the work before the hottest part of the day. One of the gnomes came forward and asked if he could make a watering system for his own garden. Since he was brilliant in his ability to make it work, Carroll asked him if he'd make a way for others to have the same system. And he would get paid for his labor.

"I meant to ask you, how do you pay a faerie? I mean, it's not like they can carry around money or even a credit card. I'm sure you guys take care of that in some way." He told her they did, but they paid in items like string for thatches for their roof. Or dried bark for their doors. "I like that. But we need to come up with something very special for them. Something that will make them the envy of all the others. I have noticed they love to make their fellow workers jealous of things."

"I think that's what they live for." They were headed back to the house when he thought of something they might well like. "Did you know that they drink tea? I'm sure you noticed all of them drink all the time, but it's sweetened with honey. What if we were to give them a bit of a honeycomb? Something they'd use, but also something that for them is hard to come by. I have a friend that has bees. It might be something we can think about."

"I love that idea. I know your mom produces honey too. I did get to use what she gave me the next morning. Even the grape tasting one is very good." Carroll told Hanna that the man, Mr. Banks, had been raising bees and getting honey for decades. That his mom had helped him start his own hive. "It's the best I've ever eaten next to your mom's. Morgan told me he doesn't use chemicals either for the flowers he grows for the flavors. That is an excellent idea."

"Are we going to be giving any to Mary and Pix?" Hanna thought that might not be such a good idea. "Oh? Why, if you don't mind me asking?"

"They should have come to us when she first captured them. I know they said they didn't want to bother us when it was only the single seed, but as you pointed out, a single seed can produce a lot of flowers. And now, not only will we have to destroy the plant that she more than likely grew, but the seeds that go with it. I think that's a good thing they did, but they should have come forward sooner."

"That's good thinking. I like that." She laughed when he did. "I hope that if we were to have children, you'd be the one that would be there for punishments. I'd be so bad at it, finding some way to reward them no matter what they did."

"Do you want children with me?" They'd not

really talked about it, but he told her he really did. "I've thought of all kinds of things about our children. Things I don't think as a human I'd have to worry about. Like, will they be cats? Will they be at least part human? This isn't something a person goes into lightly, is it?"

"They don't. Does that mean you don't want to have children? It's your body, and I have no trouble whatsoever if you don't." She smiled at him. "Did that sound like I was being too nice? I mean it. I do. I'd never force anything on you that you didn't want to do. Ever."

"I want children with you." He picked her up and swung her around the room. He would have taken care that she would not have his child if that was the way she wanted it, but he was thrilled to death that she wanted kids too. His mom would be happy as well, he thought.

After settling down at the desk again, making notes on the things they'd done at the meetings, he thought about Hanna and children. Carroll wasn't sure there was anything more beautiful than seeing a woman you loved heavy with a child. When his mom showed up, Hanna told her what they'd been talking about, including the honey, and she was happy with both ideas.

"Now we take care of the Mission women. I have had her fired from the school. I know I didn't have any proof, but I spoke with one of the many board members, and they did it immediately. Her sister, Rachel, is also going to lose her job. The people of this town know what it is they have in us, and they're willing to do just about anything to keep us safe and happy." Mom asked him what he wanted to do to the women. "And your brothers want in on this as well. When they heard about what they did to Pix's mate, they were as angry as they were when they found out I was a target. We need to get this taken care of sooner rather than later. I don't want her coming back on us again."

"Good. I have a plan." He listened to what Hanna had to say, and it was brilliant. Even his brothers couldn't find fault in it, which was saying a lot. They didn't want anyone to get their comeuppance unless they did it. But Hanna, once again, had it under control. "We start tomorrow after the FDA in charge of this area now goes to see them. That's the best way. Pile their woes up high, so they make a big mistake, then we go for the throat."

"Throat? All right. I'm in." Mom laughed. "I think your sweet little mate here is more devious than I am. I'm going to love working with her on things."

"I'm glad. But Mom, when you two are plotting something that I'm going to have done to me, will you at least give me a heads up? I want to be able to get my will in order." They all laughed, and he wasn't certain they were humoring him or laughing with him. Carroll decided to be on his best behavior from now on.

~*~

Rachel answered the door. She hated people, and

today was making her like them even less. The only person in the world that seemed to understand her was Blanche, and she couldn't stand her either.

Blanche had been a spinster all her life. Even when men came around courting her, she would blow them off in favor of tormenting others. It had been a sore spot in her married life with her brother until they moved in with one another to save money. Then she got it. There was a lot of fun to be had when you did things to others.

"Mrs. Mission, I presume?" Rachel asked him what the fuck he wanted. "Such a nice disposition you have. I was warned you might be nasty to me. Well, this is going to just make your day. You have twenty-four hours to get all the chemicals out of your yard, including the toxic waste buried somewhere out there. There will be a crew coming on board as soon — " The man turned, and a large truck pulled up in front of her home. "Well, they're here now. In addition to helping with the removal, you will need to find yourself someplace else to live. The land and the house here are no longer fit to live in. You'll assist them in the removal and then pay them when it's — "

"What the bloody fuck are you talking about?" He handed her several sheets of paper, the top one showing the word *contaminated*. Trying to shove it back at him, she felt her temper rise up, which really wasn't saying all that much. It seemed to be on a hair-trigger all the time nowadays. "I'm not doing shit with this stuff. We live here. What the hell am I supposed to do if I were to leave? Nothing, that's what. Because I'm not leaving here unless it's in a body bag."

"That can be arranged too if you wish." She wasn't sure she'd heard him right. The mumbled threat had been said while he was turning away. "These men will help you pack your things into boxes they're providing for you. The only things you can remove from here are things that are not paper, metal, cloth, or food. Those will have to be inspected for any kind of contraband you might have wrapped into them before they are released."

"Well, that's everything, now, isn't it?" He laughed, and she glared at him. "Like I said, I'm not leaving anyway. So take this and shove it up your ass."

There were two women walking up her sidewalk when she shoved the man out of her way. Rachel was going to have a stroke if she didn't get rid of these people. She'd already been terminated today, and she didn't need anything else making her pissed. Blanche came from the backyard just as she was ready to pounce on the women.

"What the hell are you doing here?" She asked Blanche who they were. "That one there is the FDA person I was telling you about. The other is Morgan. She's been the one fucking up our plans to make sure we have better gardens than she does."

"You have a single tree, and it's sad looking. The other one is in need of some major watering, as well as being put into the soil. The poor things. Nothing more than that. Even the herbs you have in your yard were sickly. Now we know why. You've been pouring chemicals into the earth and making this entire area sick with it. You should be ashamed of yourself." Rachel asked Morgan why she even cared. "Because every part of this earth is precious. When you mess up one place, you hurt all the areas around it. The birds that land in your trees, the insects that are eaten by the birds. You've damaged a lot of creatures with your actions."

"Who cares? It's not like I'm in anyone else's yard. And even if a little of this shit did leak down into the neighbor's yard, what did it do? Nothing. They have flowers and trees that shade their land. You should grow the fuck up, lady. No one cares about a little patch of earth that hasn't anything going for it." The man that had shown up first ordered her and Blanche to be arrested. "What the hell? What for?"

"You just admitted you did the damage to the dirt here voluntarily. Even if that's not anything that will stick in a court of law, it's enough to get you out of here while we do some serious looking around. Like for a gun. Do you happen to know where it is? It would save us a lot of time and effort if you told me." Rachel looked at her sister-in-law, then at the shed that she had put the gun in. "Well now, isn't that just about the nicest thing. Officers, I think we might have some telling evidence in the shed over there."

"Wait just a damned minute here. Wait. I had nothing to do with her shooting at that woman over there. She said she wanted her out of the picture, and I just went along with her because—well, I just did. We're family." Rachel was jerked around and taken to the cruiser. Things were not going according to plan, and she was going to take care of that shit right now. "I'll give you all the money you want if you just let me go. There isn't any way whatever you have on me is going to stick. The people around here are afraid of me. And rightly so. Just let me go to get a good head start, and you can have whatever you find in the way of cash in the house."

"Are you trying to bribe me?" She said she was only offering him an opportunity. "Which I guess is one way you'd put it. But no, I don't want to let you go. Nor am I going to be afraid of you."

As she was being read her rights, Rachel kept asking why she was being arrested. This was getting old. The only reason she had stayed in this little town was because it offered her a free place to live while sponging off Blanche. People didn't understand how hard it was for the elderly to be alone. Oh, she thought, that was a good one. She was going to use that as her defense when they took her to court. Rachel was still thinking about how to make herself seem less like she was a strong sixty-year-old and more like a feeble-minded elder when the woman from the neighboring farm came over to talk to her.

"I want you to know that once you're out of jail, you're going to have to move on. This land will take a while to heal, and we'd just as soon you do not live here to mess it up again." Rachel asked her what she was supposed to do then, laying the feeble on as thick as she could. "I could care less. But you will, from now on, tell the truth about everything asked of you."

The feeling of dread came over her, along with the knowledge that the woman's last words were not just her *asking* her to be truthful but saying she would have to be that way for the rest of her life. Staggering to the cruiser, she sat down and looked at the officer, then at the woman.

"She hexed me." The cop laughed and told her that she more than likely did just that. "I don't want to tell the truth. No one wants to tell the truth all the time."

"In most cases, I'd have to agree with you, but in this case, where you've pissed off one of the nicest, most generous people I know, I'm thinking she's out to make sure you don't get out of jail none too soon." They both watched as Morgan, or whatever her name was, moved to where Blanche was standing. The same look, the look of dread, fell over Blanche's eyes when Morgan walked away. "Yes, ma'am, I think this is going to be a good day for a great many people. At least some closure for some.

Did you kill your husband, Rachel? I've been wondering that since he came up being shot while out hunting. Your husband never hunted a day in his life, and there he was, shot in the head by some unknown. Were you the unknown?"

"Yes. He was in my way of getting things just the way I wanted them. Then I found out the fucking prick had changed the beneficiary of his insurance that I was counting on to his cousin. What the hell would make him do that?" It hurt her to answer him. The truth be damned. "Don't talk to me. I don't want you to ask me another damned question. Do you hear me?"

Rachel sat in the back seat, plotting. She didn't know how to make any of the ideas she had running through her head work—she couldn't even lie to herself now. When the cruiser Blanche was in took off, she sat there thinking of her lot in life. And again, not being able to lie, she knew whatever came her way, it was simply because she'd caused it. Her life right now was a train wreck, and there was no getting out of the way of it.

The station house was ready for her, it seemed. Not only was she given a cell of her own, but she also didn't see Blanche anywhere. Not that she wanted to see her or to even talk to her. Telling her the truth would piss her off, and Rachel was sure they both had enough to deal with at the moment. Sitting on the cot, she looked around and saw a bug or something sitting in the high windowsill. Standing up, she nearly hit it when he spoke to her.

"Isn't it just grand that there is even sunshine coming in here to greet you? I mean, I know you didn't go out much, but it's a glorious thing to have sunlight streaming on your face when you're down. Don't you think?" She asked it who it was. "You know what I am. You've killed enough of my kind to know we're faeries. And since you murdered my mate, I've been given the job of keeping you company. Lady Morgan said, so long as I don't harm you, where people can see at least, I could torment you as much as I wanted. I think I'm going to enjoy this a great deal."

The first thing he did was start to sing. It wasn't so bad at first, hearing that old bar song that counted beer bottles backwards. But after he did it for what seemed hours, he started the fucking song over. Starting at one thousand and going again and again.

"Please, will you just shut up?" He didn't. In fact, Rachel was sure that he was singing louder. "Shut the fuck up."

It was dinner time when he got to what she hoped was the last number. Her head finally got the reprieve that she'd been wanting. Then he started singing a ditty about a lovely bunch of coconuts or some shit. Christ, she was going to kill someone if she ever got out of here.

Chapter 6

Morgan put the book down that she'd been reading. It had been so long since she'd had any time to pick up anything to do for herself. It had taken her eyes a minute to remember how to read. That, she thought, was pretty sad. When Leslie came into the room and sat down across from her, she waited him out. Of all the boys, he was the biggest thinker. And took the longest time to come up with an answer.

"I've been thinking about the land the couple owned. I was told downtown that you have already purchased it." She said the people at the courthouse had contacted her that morning. "Yes. That's what I was told. I'd like to have it. The house and the little bit of property that surrounds it. Unless you have something else in mind for it."

"No. Other than razing the house, nothing. What

did you have in mind?" He said he was going to build himself a store. "Sounds good. What sort of store? I mean, things from here to resell, or were you thinking something less meat and potatoes?"

"I want to be able to have a resell store, but nothing to do with what we have here. It would be a place that someone looking for a sink or some kind of cabinet could go and get a good price on it. I know there are hardware places online that people can get that from, but these won't be new items. It will be things I can either pick up cheap or something that someone no longer wants and just tells me to come and get it." Morgan told him that was a great idea. "I have three of the faeries to help me. They have the ability to fix electrical things without any fuss. I know it's cheating, but I think it will help a lot of people that just don't have the means to get something brand new."

"The money you make from the sales, what are your plans for that? You must have this all worked out, knowing you." He told her. "Good. I like that too. Using all the money to purchase more things is a good way to keep things in inventory. One of the things I know people have trouble getting is a washer and dryer. Those are needed in just about every home I know of here."

"Jake, he's one of the faeries, told me he knows where things are being dumped. Things like washers and dryers. We could do a cleanup kind of action while we're fixing things. Also, he said he could work on cars. Give someone a leg up by giving them transportation." Morgan was liking his plan more and more. But she wasn't going to help him. She needed to let them take things off her plate, not add to it. Smiling at him, she told him what she'd been thinking. "Good. I wasn't going to offer, but I do feel better with you knowing you aren't going to help. I love that you're more rested and less stressed than you'd been before. You seem so much more relaxed."

"I feel it too. I love Hanna helping me out. She does fuss at me when she thinks I'm overdoing it. But she does it in a way that doesn't make me feel like she's being bossy." Leslie said she was bossy to him. "Because you, my dear boy, are afraid of her."

"I am. And of you too, if you want the truth. Not so much afraid, but I don't want to disappoint you. I think all of us are, a great deal, afraid of disappointing you in some way or another." She said that was very sweet of him, but she'd never felt disappointed in any of them. "I find myself feeling like I've messed up sometimes, not with you, but in general. Also, I'm a little afraid of my mate coming along, and she's going to be a disappointment to all of us. It's like having Hanna here has set the bar for the rest of us. She's going to be hard to match, don't you think?"

"No matter what sort of person she is or how much

she is or is not like Hanna, we'll all love her because she loves you. Leslie, she is going to be your other half. The only way we could not like her if she was to harm you in any way. Physically or mentally. I don't see that happening, however. Do you?" He said he didn't. "Good. The project you have in mind is a very good one. Noble, I'd say. Helping out the others as we have over the years will come back to us tenfold. That's one of the reasons I was to be your mom, you know. To teach each of you how to blend in with those around you, and to help you understand that helping people less fortunate than you is something that will always be welcomed."

"Thanks, Mom."

Leslie left her soon after. Getting up, she went to the shelves to find herself something else to read. There were plenty to chose from. Some of them had been in the house when her parents had died. Those, she knew, were nothing that they'd ever read, but only for show.

The knock at the door had her getting up again. It was almost too much to be this relaxed, she thought with a grin. Opening the door, she was surprised to find someone there she didn't know. Anyone coming onto this property had to know just how to get past the gates and needed to be invited. She hadn't done either for this person.

"May I help you?" The girl, woman she supposed, looked at her. Morgan could tell she was confused.

Dazed even. Asking her again if she needed anything, the woman looked at her, terrified.

"I don't know who I am. Or how I got here." Helping her into the house, Morgan could smell fresh blood. As soon as she got her to sit on the couch, she called in her boys. Hanna was the first to arrive. "Do I know you? I seem to think I should, but— I can't remember anything. Not even how I got to the door."

"Her mind is blank. There isn't even a memory of her walking up the stairs to your door. And the wounds on her look like something was burnt into her flesh." Morgan told her it was from shock treatment. "You mean they still do that?"

"I don't know. But that's what I'd say happened here." Marley brought with him a black bag. He'd been dabbling in being a full-time doctor for a few months and had pulled out his working bag at some point. She told him what she and Hanna had figured out. "She got here without any alarms being raised. That concerns me."

"I should have told you this earlier. Tellus was here a couple of days ago and put in reinforcements. She didn't want anyone here being hurt with those women running around." Marley helped the woman roll to her side so he could have a look at her wounds. "You're right. These have been made with some sort of electrical probe or something similar. They were more than— Look. There are marks on the back of her head as well. That would explain the total loss of memory."

After getting her settled in one of the bedrooms, two faeries were chosen to keep an eye on her and answer any questions she might have if it came to that. On their way back downstairs, Marley told them both what had happened with Tellus. She had not just reinforced the perimeter, but she had reinforced the magic that made it so no one with ill-will could enter without a long and painfully slow death. While it wasn't likely that was what had happened to the younger woman, it could have been. Calling to one of the faeries, she asked them to see what they could find out about the woman.

"I'm going to go too. As my leopard." She asked Carroll if that was necessary. "I think it might be. I'll be able to track her movements since she came onto this land. I could see if she walked through the gate or was transported here in some other way. There are any number of things that would explain how she got here. Not why, but at least we'd have an idea of how."

"All right. But be careful." He kissed her on the cheek, then Hanna when she told him she'd kick his ass if he got hurt. Morgan was beginning to see why the boys were afraid of their sister-in-law.

Hanna spoke in softer tones, never raising her voice, but she did make her point when she did. Even when she smiled while saying it, there wasn't any doubt she meant what she said. Morgan would bet anything

that Carroll knew it too. Smiling to herself, she asked
Hanna if she wanted to wait here for Carroll.

"I would like that. Also, I have a couple of things
I'd like to ask you. Nothing earth-shattering, but about
this bit of magic I discovered I had this morning." As
they were headed down the stairs, Flan, another faerie,
stayed outside the room the wounded woman was in
while Hanna told her about the magic. "I can pull from
the earth. Nothing surprising there. I think that is where
most of this comes from. But when I touch something
deeper in the soil, like a tree with long deep roots, I can
almost see what is beneath it, like the bugs and stuff that
burrow there. Also, I can tell if the roots are doing well.
Then if they're not, I have the ability to give it a little of
myself to heal it."

"That doesn't sound all that problematic." She
told her there was more. "Okay, you're a lead me along
the path. Good. What is the problem then? I'm sure it's
all right."

"The trees talk to me." Morgan had thought that
was what she was going to say. But it seemed to upset
Hanna more than she thought it should have. Before she
could tell her it was good to be able to speak to the trees
and other things of nature, she continued. "There are
seven people on your land right now that are digging
into the soil. The ground, who talks to the trees, said he
doesn't know what they're looking for, but it's hurting

the earth to have them leaving their trash and other things lying around. Gasoline is also being used to dig."

"Do you know where?" She told her that with a map of the land, she could not only tell her where they were but what they were doing at that very moment. "How long have they been there?"

"This is their second month. I asked why no one had reported it before now, and I was told there hadn't been anyone to speak to the trees before. I think I told you I can talk to all the animals, didn't I?" She nodded, wondering what could possibly be going on out there. "Well, one of the animals that lives on that end of your property is coming here, so I can get as much answered as I can. Apparently, I'm the go-to person now when there are issues with the earth and things growing around here."

"Are you upset?" Hanna shook her head and said she was more freaked out than anything. "I would think I'd be as well. When is this animal set to arrive?"

"He's in the yard now."

Going out back, there stood the biggest buck she'd ever seen. Morgan would bet that he had forty points to his rack, and it was his pride. To be living here and not being harmed would account for the size of his rack.

"Do you want anything answered by him? I was just going to let him tell me what he's found. By the way, he is called Bucky. His father, older than him, of course, is Buck. He's even bigger than this one is."

Hanna spoke with the buck, and Morgan wondered if she knew she was speaking whatever language the buck was speaking. To her, it sounded like gibberish. Grunts and sounds that only another animals could understand. But apparently, the buck could not only understand what Hanna was telling him but also had a good grasp of what was going on at the other end of the land. She wanted to ride out there right now and see what it was about but didn't.

Morgan used to charge right into whatever was going on and damn the information that might help her when she got there. In the years since then, she'd learned there were always two sides to every story, that things were not always as cut and dried as they seemed. Her favorite one was, nothing was ever as simple as it was being told to her. There were turns and corners all over the place. Navigating them was what she'd learned from working here on this land.

"Buck said they're digging around the mountain looking for shiny stones. He doesn't know what sort of colors they're bringing up, but he is sure that some of them are green. It's about the only color he's familiar with." Hanna laughed. "I was just thinking we need to have classes with the animals to tell them things they're never going to learn by being whatever they are. Anyway, they've been there for a few new moons. And they come and go off the property nightly. He has followed them out of the land to the edge of the property, but no further. I think we should send out a troll to move them along. And if that doesn't work, then we call the police. Buck said we should get whatever it is they're finding, as they're very excited when they dig it up. Do you think it might be emeralds and diamonds?"

"At one time, long ago, it was speculated that there might well be a diamond mine around here close by. As for emeralds, I wouldn't know. But I'm sure if you can picture one of them in your mind, you can ask the trees to find out what it is they're digging up." Hanna told her she was brilliant and kissed her on the cheek. When she put her hands to the tree next to them, she told her what he was saying. "They do have emeralds. He thanks you for the visual. Buck said he'd think of what other things they were bringing up and let us know." Morgan was enjoying this. Not having the people on her land, but the way things were being broadcasted to her, so she wasn't forever having to be on top of things. When Hanna smiled at her, she started smiling back. "The troll showed up just now, and it's mayhem there. Not only are they throwing today's finds at him, but also their bottled water and anything else they can touch. They're armed too, apparently, but aren't shooting. That's good. I think it would only piss him off more and get the troll hurt too."

In less time than it would have taken her to get to the other side of the property, the people were gone, their mess cleaned up, and most if not all the gems piled into a neat pile. Hanna asked her what she wanted to be done with the gems.

"I have no idea. It's not like I knew they were there. Why don't we have them brought here? We'll see what they're worth and go from there. Leslie is starting up a new project, and perhaps he can use whatever money we can get for them for his startup." Hanna thought that was a great idea. "Thanks. I have them on occasion."

Even having them brought there was a good deal easier than she thought it would have been. The faeries were so happy to gather them up that they even made a bag the gems could be put into, then carried by the lot of them. She and Hanna were in the kitchen, enjoying a nice cup of tea when Carroll joined them still as his cat.

She was tossed out of a moving vehicle about two miles from here. Her coming up our drive was unnoticed because she had been coming through one of the gaps in the fencing. I've had a couple of faeries take some of the others with them to go along the fencing and see if there are any more gaps. She didn't bother anything as she came through. Nor on her trip up to the house. She is correct, however — she has been dazed like this since she was literally tossed from the car. Carroll went to their home to change and then returned with some things he'd picked up. "I don't have any idea what these are from, but they look like receipts. Not from anywhere I can make out."

Morgan picked one of the pieces of paper up. "This is for gasoline. I had no idea it was getting so expensive. But it's one from about twenty miles north of here." Carroll said he'd go and figure out what he could. "Take one or more of your brothers with you in the event you need back up. Not that I don't think you can take care of yourself, but we have no idea what we're up against right now."

"All right. Will you stay with my mom? I don't think anything will happen here, but I'd feel better if the two of you were together." Neither of them answered Carroll, but he seemed to be satisfied with that. When he was gone, Hanna looked at her with a strange smile.

"I don't know if he's being overly protective or just trying to keep us out of trouble. Not that I think I cause him too much in the way of trouble, but we might not ever know what we can do when we get our minds made up about something." Morgan really liked this girl. She was honest and refreshing. Especially since she'd been around men most of her life, Morgan was enjoying having another female around all the time. "I think when this is all over with the Mission sisters, you and I have to go out on the town. Stir up some trouble and see what we can get ourselves into. I'm not a partier or anything like that, but it might be fun."

"I'd like that."

The young woman joined them while they were arguing over what sort of ice cream went with pie. Hanna said whipped cream went on pie, ice cream on cake. Morgan found herself disagreeing simply for the sake of arguing.

The woman sat down and asked for something to drink, and Hanna got it for her. "How are you feeling?"

"I don't know. But I do know my first name. It's Venetia. Other than that, I don't know. Bits and pieces come to me, but nothing I can figure out. How did you know my mind was empty?" Hanna explained to her what she'd done. "Do you think you can see my memories now and perhaps make sense of them?"

"I can try." When Hanna got up again and gave a glass of juice to Venetia, she sat back down. "You work in a law firm, I think. You might have just been there, but you seem to not be intimidated by the place. I can't tell which one, but I can see there are all kinds of law books in the room you remember."

"That's right. I do work there. I was there in the morning. What's the date?" Morgan told her. "Yes, three days ago. I was going someplace else that day. This is nice. Thank you for your help."

"No problem. We'll take it as we go. My husband is looking around for more clues right now. He is going to see what happened when you were dropped off." She said she didn't remember that. "It's all right. Don't force anything. It'll come when it comes."

Morgan talked to the two girls, enjoying their company more than she did anything. Finding out information was vital, but Morgan thought it would be terrible news and she'd lose her new friend. She'd never, in all her life, dreamed of having a girlfriend to hang out with, and right now, she was enjoying the two that were here today.

~*~

"What sort of news have you heard? I mean, any dead bodies lying alongside the road? Venetia was nothing but trouble from the moment we hired her. I told you she wasn't like her father. I doubt she was easy even as a child. Nope. Nothing at all like him." Benson told him he was sorry, but he thought they could recruit her. "Fat lot of good that did us trying. She was working for the Feds from day one. If I didn't know any better, I'd say she wasn't even an attorney. But her knowledge of it is off the charts good."

"I've spoken to her *mother*." He did quotation marks when he said mother, and Colton had to smile. Betty had been a suitable helpmate for Venetia's fake father, Sheppard after his wife was out of the picture. Then when he'd stepped out of line one too many times, he'd been taken care of as well. It had been easier still to slip in a father figure like Sherman before Venetia had any memory of her biological parents. Sherman would have done anything they asked of him at the time, and they played that card whenever they needed someone killed or even put away.

"Venetia's mother, someone they didn't know well, had been killed the night they killed Roman. All they knew about her was that she'd been a real beauty—so was her daughter—and that she'd had a bit of magic. No one seemed to know if Venetia had gotten any of it, and Colton liked it that way. The less of that shit going around, the better.

"Betty is saying once Venetia left the house that morning, she never heard from her again. I'm assuming she'll have to go as well. Betty has been a great asset for us, you know." Colton asked if the police had been called yet. "No. She was leaving town, and it's not occurred to anyone yet that she might well be hurt. I thought that played well into giving us more time."

"She has, and you're right. She has to go. I'm worried now she's attached herself to the kid. She'll not want anything to happen to her if we find out she's a squealer. Sherman, he was a good Joe right up until the time he wasn't, then there was no stopping him from doing stupid shit. He never could keep his mouth shut when it was necessary. It was a right shame that he had to go and get himself a mistress." Colton laughed. "Turned out she was the smarter of the two of them. Figured out quicker than he did what we were doing here."

Other than making money hand over foot, they were bringing in all kinds of shit without using any of the usual channels to make it happen. Colton couldn't remember the last time he'd been in a courtroom to work. And he was sure Benson hadn't been around them much either.

They were buying drugs and reselling them, which took up a great deal of their time. Bringing in illegal aliens that were needed to repackage their dope was another full-time job. They'd have to be trained, then slapped around a bit to show them who was boss. Also, they had a nice little thing going with the prostitution ring that was growing larger by the day.

"I called the locals when I was leaving the town we dropped her body in. I told them I thought I saw a body on the side of the road. When asked how come I didn't stop, I told them I was terrified of being involved." Benson laughed. "They bought it all. Even the part where I said she was didn't seem to be breathing. She wasn't when I kicked her to the side."

"Too bad that had to happen. I mean, Venetia sure was a looker. I had big plans for her. You did use your little lesson learner on her, didn't you? I don't want to know how much fun you had with it, but you did burn any memories she might well have had about us, right?" Benson said he had, and he did have fun. "Yes, I suppose you would. However, we do need an attorney to make us look legitimate. While she was a looker, Venetia fit the bill. But she had to get her nose into things that didn't concern her. Just like Honey, Sherman's mistress did. Who the hell names their kid after bee shit?"

"Who knows if that was even her real name? But she's gone now, so we don't have to fuck with her either." They were running low on people they could trust. Mostly it was the people that were supposed to be working for them. However, there were a few still coming out of college that could be brought in. Colton just didn't want to have to fuck with it. "We should watch the news. I don't know if they'll put anything about Venetia on the news here, but it's hard to tell."

They both watched it at the bar down the street. The place made a mean sub, and he was just generous enough to pay for his and Benson's dinner. Nothing was on the news, but that really wasn't a surprise. They were an entire state away from where the drop had been made.

Just as he was getting ready to pay up and go home, a tall man came into the bar with three of the biggest men he'd ever seen.

"They look like models. Don't you think?" Colton nodded. "They're probably lost or something. No one just comes in here without a good reason. It's our place, you know."

"I doubt they'd care. Look how they carry

themselves like they know they're all tough and shit and don't give a shit who knows it. I'm betting cousins or something." Benson said brothers. When they sat down at the bar and looked around, Colton felt his balls tighten up around his ass when one of them pinned him with his eyes. "Do we know them?"

"I don't think so. That does make me wonder what you did to him in another life. He looks like he could murder you where you sit." That's the exact feeling he got. And he didn't like it. "Why don't we get out of here and get home? I have some stuff I have to take care of in the morning, and it's going to take most of that time up."

Just as they were walking past the men, the one that had come in first turned to face him. There wasn't even a hint of a smile on his face. No look of any kind, as a matter of fact. This was a man you'd not play cards with or any other game of chance. The man stopped him by putting his foot out.

"Venetia is still alive." Benson asked him what he'd said. "I said Venetia is still alive. In fact, she's talking to the police now. It's really too bad you didn't get out of your car and check on her before leaving the scene of the crime."

"Colton?" Colton, feeling exposed, angrily told the younger man to get out of his way. He didn't know what he was talking about. But Benson didn't move, and the man looked at him. "I don't know what you're talking about, young man. Leave us alone. We don't know a Venetia Hamm."

"I never said her last name. You should have left her alone. And her father. Not the man who raised her, but the one that sired her. Have you all your ducks in a row, Mr. Colton Henderson?" The man laughed. "I'd say you should seek a better attorney than you are. You're going to need to have your will properly made out and filed. I'm coming for you."

Colton was out the door and in his car before he felt like his asshole could sneak out a fart. Not to mention that his cock coming unstuck from his balls was a painful reminder of the man searing him with a look. Christ, it was like talking to the devil himself in there. Looking over at Benson, he asked him if he'd been hit—his nose was bleeding.

"So is yours." Looking in the mirror, he saw the three men behind him, in the back seat of all places. But when he turned, he didn't see anything. "What the hell was that? They knew too much, Colton. Way too much for my happiness. And how do they know she was still alive?"

"That's the least of our problems. He knew my name. He also knew that Venetia wasn't Sherman's daughter." Colton was scared shitless. He didn't know what the hell was going on or how this man knew so much, but he wanted answers. "Go back to where you dropped her and see what you can find out. Maybe she's really dead, and he's just fishing."

"He knew her name too. Christ, and I gave him a clue that I did actually know her."

Colton wasn't going to think about how much the man had told them in a few short seconds. Like he'd— Suddenly, he stopped thinking and looked at Benson.

"What? What did you figure out?"

"He's like her dad. Venetia's father. He read our minds. And while he got some information from doing it, we can rest assured he's not all that good at it yet. He hurt us when he did it. People who are good at it, you don't even know they're doing that shit. So whatever he got, it's just the surface stuff." Benson said he didn't know what that meant. "He wasn't able to get deep into our minds. He could only rape our minds, I think it's called. From now on, we'll be careful about that. We should be able to feel him when he tries again. At least that's what Roman told me. We'll have to think of stupid shit. Like the ABCs or math things. That will mess him up." At least he hoped so.

Roman Burgeon had been something, but not human. He would never tell him what he was, not even when he took his life. He wouldn't even tell him who he'd been talking to about their business. Since he was dead and the wife out of the picture, the baby was there for Colton to steal. His plan had been to sell her off, but now that he thought about it, Colton was sure the baby, even back then, wouldn't allow him to do that. It was like she knew she had to grow up and hurt him in some way. He wished more and more every day that he'd just killed her too. He might have been better off than he was right now. Damn it all to fuck and back. He hated shit like this.

Chapter 7

Hanna sat at the little table waiting on Blanche to be brought out so she could talk to her. There were others visiting their family members here today, and she took note of the ones that were genuinely innocent and the ones that should have been sent to a bigger prison well before landing in the jail here.

The things she could do with her magic now was empowering. Not only did she figure something out daily, but she was getting a handle on the powers she needed to help Morgan out the most. Carroll had told her yesterday about the upcoming street fair the town was having and the things his family would be involved in. She was sort of glad Blanche, as well as her sister-in-law, weren't going to be around to mess it up.

Apparently, over the years, the Mission sisters would set up a booth of their own and hand out pamphlets.

Nothing that anyone wanted — they were just more of the same things, saying that the town was going to come to ruin because of Morgan and her leap. Hanna laughed a little, thinking of the different versions she'd heard as to why Morgan had called her land "leap" and not ranch or any of the other names that she could have used. Some knew the meaning, but very few of them cared.

"What do you want?" She's missed Blanche being brought to her and smiled at the other woman. This was going to be difficult for the older woman. At least she thought it might be. "I don't want to see you. You and that other bitch have caused me enough trouble as it is. Why don't you just go home and leave us decent people alone?"

"Yesterday, when you and Rachel were picked up, you were brought here. Rachel was taken to the hospital sometime in the middle of the night. She was suffering from chest pains, she told the officers." Blanche sort of slumped in her seat as if she knew what was coming next. "The doctors did all they could to save her. She, as I'm sure you know, was a diabetic and had heart problems. Carrying around that extra weight had made her heart work too hard. She passed away earlier this morning. I'm sorry for your loss."

She didn't say anything for a while, just sat there staring at her. Hanna was sure she wasn't seeing her but thinking. When she blinked several times in a row,

Blanche finally started speaking.

"I'd like to blame this all on you and that Morgan person, but that would just be stupid. Rachel had been told to lose weight and to watch what she ate. She, of course, thought she was smarter than a doctor. She might well have been—she sure told me enough that she was." Blanche laughed a little. "I don't know what to feel right now."

"Understandable. Did she have any family aside from you out there someplace?" Blanche told her she had a daughter, as well as a son. "Do you know if they kept in contact with her? Or you, for that matter since you would be their aunt."

"No. I've only seen them a handful of times. I doubt very much they'd care that Rachel was dead either. I think they might have written her out of their lives before they left home all those years ago." Blanche asked her if her death had been quick. Hanna told her it had been. "Good. For as much as I didn't like her, I don't think I would have wanted her to suffer. She and my brother weren't well suited. But that's water under the bridge, I suppose. What happens now?"

"I don't know, to be honest with you. Nothing can be done until we notify her next of kin. Even if what you say is true, they'll need to be told their mother has died." Blanche nodded. "There are a couple of other things I need to inform you about. First of all, your home has been condemned. Not my doing, but because of the black mold that has grown through it. It's a wonder, the inspector said, that neither of you got seriously ill from it."

"We knew that too. Rachel would get into some breathing issues, and the doctor at the emergency room told her that she was breathing it in. We fobbed him off like we do most other people telling us we're doing something wrong or whatever. I guess you can understand that we don't care for people in general." Hanna told her she got that about the two of them. "Yeah, I guess you would. I guess you're going to tell me I'm going to have a court hearing about shooting at Morgan."

"We found the bullet you fired at her and missed. The evidence is very telling that you are the one that loaded the gun. Rachel's prints were on it too, but you fired it last." She said she had. Hanna didn't understand this. Blanche was being nice. Sort of what she'd think an elderly woman would be like. "What's going on here? Why are you calmly taking what I'm telling you and not calling me names like you did yesterday? You didn't suddenly have a change of heart, have you?"

"No." She laughed again. This time it seemed to be sort of manic. "When you told me that Rachel had died, I sort of half expected that I guess. She gets all fired up and then has to sit for a spell to get her heart to slow down. But after that, I realized that other than her kids,

I got no one to mourn my passing when I go on. After that—it was like every bad deed I did just flashed before my eyes. Do you suppose that's what people mean when they say that? That all your misdeeds flash by, not your whole life?"

"I don't know." Hanna thought if anyone was going to have a lot of bad deeds to flash before her eyes, it would be this woman. Just skimming her mind, she could see that she'd killed before. "They'll allow you to go to her funeral if you want. Like I said, we have no plans as yet until we talk with her kids."

"There is a number for the girl. Her name was…let me think a minute. But there is a phone number for her on the desk in her room. I don't know how you're going to get it with the house being closed off like it is. I think there is an email address for her son too, but I couldn't tell you if that is right either." She put her finger to her head and closed her eyes. "I can almost see that girl's name. Nothing like her momma nor me. Either of them, for that matter. Allison. That's it. Named after my grandmother. The boy's name is Butch. Nickname, I think, but I don't know for sure. They'd be in their twenties by now, I guess. Not kids at all."

Without going to the home, she had all the information she needed. But Hanna didn't get up and leave just yet. She had a feeling there was more to this with Blanche than she was letting on about. When nothing more seemed to be forthcoming, Hanna started to dig deeper when she spoke again.

"I have a daughter too." That wasn't at all what she had expected to hear and asked her if she could contact her. "You can try. It's doubtful she'll care either. I've not thought of her in decades. She'd be about fifty now, I guess. I had her when I was nothing more than a kid myself. That's why she would be so much older than her cousins. Meredith was already in high school when my brother started having kids. But I raised her right up until she decided I was holding her back from life. Not sure what that meant even now."

Again, Hanna didn't either but figured she'd work on finding her as well. After getting what she could from Blanche, she asked her if she needed anything. That brought tears to the older woman's weathered cheeks, and Hanna wasn't sure what she'd done.

"After all I've done to that family of yours—I know that now, that they're your family—you'd still ask me if you can help me. And you mean it too, don't you?" Hanna told her she did mean it. "I thought you would. I have me some money in the bank. I'd like for you to make me some funeral arrangements. Whatever you think is the least expensive. I'm sure that's what you did for Rachel. That's good. It's what I would have done even though I think there is some money from her insurance or something."

"I can do that. Do you have a place picked out where you wish to be buried?" She told her if she could, next to Rachel. "I'll see what I can do. I'll come back here, Blanche, to let you know what I find out. And if I find your daughter, do you want her to come and see you?"

"No. No, I'd not want that. I'm sure she'd not want it either, but no, she doesn't need to come see me. If you find out she's been long dead, I'd not want to know that either. Just knowing she's out there, it does give me a little bit to think about." Nodding, she told her she'd do that. Her daughter wasn't dead, but she wasn't in a good place in her life either. It seemed to her that the daughter was much like her mother in that she didn't like people, nor did she have any friends. "I don't want a big marker either. Just a stone or something that says I died, and my name. Nothing fancy is what I mean. Just a little bitty stone that tells the person reading it that I died."

"I can do that." She would too. Even for Rachel, if the kids didn't. "I have to get going, Blanche. Is there anything I can do for you? Something I can make sure you get?"

"No. I don't want you to be expecting me to be like this the next time you visit me. I'll have time to get my dander up again, and I might well blast you apart. But for now, I wanted to tell you thanks for coming around. And for telling me about Rachel." Hanna told her it was her pleasure. "I'm sure it wasn't, but again, I thank you for that."

Hanna made her way to the building Carroll and his brother were working on. The house was cleaned up now, and it smelled like lavender. The smell of death had been taken away by the magic from the faeries. As soon as she saw him, Hanna hugged Carroll and found that with his arms around her, she felt better than she had in a couple of days. He didn't say anything but continued holding her.

"Blanche took it well that her sister-in-law was gone." He told her that was good. "She asked me to get some money out of her account and to set up her own funeral. I told her I'd do that too. I have a couple of names I need to contact. They both had children, did you know that?"

"I think I remember Rachel having a child, but not Blanche." She told him what she'd found out. "No. I didn't know there was a son either. I'm assuming you're going to call them?"

"I am. To let them know that she's gone. But according to Blanche, they won't care all that much." Carroll nodded and said that Blanche and Rachel had been trouble since he could remember. "This magical thing. It's coming in handy. I can trace things like people too. I didn't know it would be this helpful, but I'm getting a kick out of using it. I need something fun to do with it, however."

"Mom called here about an hour ago, looking for you. She said Venetia has her memory back and wants you to talk to her about it. She was spying on her boss and his partner, and they figured it out. She's not human, did you know that? I'm not sure she even knows." Hanna asked him how he'd figured that out. "I can smell it on her. You more than likely can as well, but since you've not had much practice at it, you might not have noticed. Also, the people that hurt her, they're being watched over by a group of faeries that will report to me anything they're doing."

"Do you think they're going to figure out she's alive and has her memory back?" Carroll told her what he'd done at the bar last night. "All right. That should make them stupid enough to try and remedy their issue of her being alive. We'll protect her, right?"

"Yes. I've also sent my brothers to the house to see if she's their mate. Leslie is the only one that hasn't been to see her yet. The others feel they need to protect her, but they aren't her mate." She looked up at him and asked why Leslie wasn't checking her out. "He told me he didn't know why, but he has a feeling she's not his mate. I don't know why he'd think that, but he told me he'd go and see her after we're done here. Mom is having us all over for dinner tonight as well. You up for it?"

"I am. I love having all this family." She laughed. "By the way, I've given my notice at the office. So, since I had all this vacation time coming to me, they're going to pay that to me if I don't come back. I expected that, but it was still sort of painful to think they didn't even try to keep me on."

"To me, that's a win-win. You're going to be here with me all the time, and you are going to be happy not having to go to work again. Not that this place doesn't keep us hopping, but you are helping so much." She thanked him. "Also, before I forget to tell you again, we're officially married according to the paperwork that was filed yesterday. When we talked the other night, you said you didn't want any sort of wedding. I'm hoping you still don't."

"No. I have all I need right here, and inviting people I barely know to come to see me hitched up with you seems sort of a waste of time and money." Carroll kissed her, pulling her body close enough to his that she could feel his erection. "You sure do know how to make a girl feel wanted, don't you?"

Laughter rang around the room they were in. Kissing her again, Carroll turned her, so she was facing the door when Leslie walked into the room they were in. He smiled, but it didn't seem to reach his eyes. She asked him what was wrong.

"This house isn't nearly big enough for what I thought I could use it for. There is the barn out back, but I was hoping to use the house." She knew his idea was a good one and asked him if he planned on being there all the time. "No. I mean, I was just going to set it up so people could call and make an appointment to come and see the things we'd have. Why? What did you have in mind?"

"Hire someone to come here and live that needs a good home. Have that person show the things that are needed by a customer." Leslie asked her where he was supposed to put the things they had. "In the barn. I'm sure there is power to the place. Even if there isn't, that's an easy fix. I'm thinking an older person would love to be able to live here and talk to people that come around. Mr. Hewitt comes to mind. He and his wife are in their fifties, I think. They've been living in that rental so long I'm sure they'd like to have something of their own."

"You mean give them the job and the house? That would be all right with me." She corrected him in what she was thinking. "I like that even better. Make it a part of their payment until they can purchase it and the business from me some time. Yes, I know the couple you're talking about. You're right. I think they'd enjoy this a great deal. Thanks."

"You keep this up, and my brothers will be coming to you for advice all the time." Hanna told Carroll she could live with that. "I thought you'd say that. And I'm glad too. I'm not sure what Leslie's plans were about being here off and on, but I think you just made it easier for him to set this up then walk away when it's complete. He's hired someone, and there is someone living here to keep people from stealing from him."

Making her way home again, she thought about the other projects she had going on with Morgan. There was plenty to do all the time, and she was sure it had been like this since her parents had died. Morgan had wanted the place to be better than it had been, and she thought the woman had gone well beyond that. She was her hero in so many ways.

~*~

Carroll stretched out. His cat had needed a run all day, and he was glad he'd been able to get away for a little while. He'd not even asked any of his brothers if they wanted to run with him. He needed just a little time to himself. However, if he could have convinced Hanna to come with him, it would have been so much better. Smiling to himself, he thought of them making love last night. Christ, the woman was wearing him out. Not that he minded all that much.

She'd been in bed when he got home late. He was as disappointed as he'd ever been. Since she'd been with him yesterday afternoon, all he'd thought about was having her naked beneath him. Finding her sound asleep made him want to cry, but he knew she was getting used to the longer hours the rest of them worked.

Going to his office, he was surprised by all the

notes on his desk from her. They were progress reports, he supposed you'd call them, on what she'd found out about Venetia. She had family around, but she didn't think the younger woman knew it. The next note was about Rachel's children and that she'd finally found them and was going to call them in the morning. But she doubted anyone would come to the funeral. He thought that was about the saddest thing he'd read in a while. He worshiped his mom.

The next note was a little more difficult to read. She'd written something, then crossed it out. Then crossed that out. He laughed when she noted on the note that she was going to start over on another sheet. He could see her thinking she needed to explain what she'd done. The note he read told him what else she'd figured out about Venetia.

"She has a sister. Older than she is by a few years. Apparently, she was spending the night with her grandparents or something and wasn't home when the baby was taken. I'm still trying to figure out what happened to make it so he was able to take the baby. And you were right, she is magical. But I don't know if you'd consider witchcraft as being non-human. Her father was some kind of big deal in that world. I'm not up on my witchcraft lingo. However, I'm thinking he isn't dead, as I first assumed. Nor is her mom. But as I said, I'm looking into that. Venetia is going to be staying with your mom for a while. They're getting along well. I hope she's Leslie's mate. I like her too." He had picked up the last note. "If you've gotten through everything, then I believe you should get your ass upstairs and wake me up screaming out a release. I need it as much as you do."

He was naked by the time he entered their bedroom. Hanna was sitting there in the middle of the bed, as naked as he was, waiting for him. Moving toward the bed, he had to smile. There was nothing about this woman that could be considered normal, and Carroll thought he'd have it no other way.

"You certainly took your time." He said he'd had to read all her notes. "Well, I guess I did leave you a lot. One thing I forgot to tell you is that I love you very much. I should have just put that on a lot of the notes and nothing else."

"I like that you leave notes to me. Especially that last one." He got into the bed with her, and she curled around him. "This makes things so much better, don't you think? Having someone in the bed when you get there. You're the very best snuggle person I've never known."

She sat up and looked at him. Thinking about what he'd said, he grinned at her. Pulling her down for a kiss, she stubbornly held fast to just staring at him. When she started to move off of him and the bed, he pulled her back to him.

"I'm thousands of years old." She didn't say anything. "I had to practice on a few women so I'd be perfect when you came to me. But I will swear to you on my mother's heart that none of them meant anything at all to me. It's been you all along that I've waited for, and you will forever be the only person I ever, ever snuggle with from here to eternity. I love you, Hanna, and only you."

"Good save." She laid her head down where he knew she could hear his beating heart. Carroll had thought about telling her it only beat for her, but he might need that one for some other time. "Are you going to keep thinking up excuses for me not to bash your head in, or are you going to make love to me?"

"Carroll?" Carroll pulled himself from his thoughts and looked at his brother. "Where the hell were you? I've been saying your name for the last five minutes. I think if you're going to stand there looking like you've just won the lottery, you should share those good vibes."

"Not on your life." It took Scout a moment to understand what he was talking about before his face turned a dark pink. Laughing at him, he asked him what he'd needed. Scout told him why he'd been looking for him. "I don't have any idea what the value of gems would be, but I do know a way we can find out. The Internet more than likely has a lot of information about their worth."

"I thought of that, and Hanna cautioned me on it. She said if we start searching that sort of stuff, people would figure it out. Something about cookies. I know what they are, but I had no idea any of the computers in our home could be used in that sort of thing." Carroll said he did know the answer to that one. "Good. I never realized, by the way, how a person can think like a criminal and not be one. Hanna is wonderful, don't get me wrong, but she's scary when she starts spouting off things that bad guys will do. She can be both the good guy and the bad without much effort in trying to outthink herself."

"I thought that as well. But she said that just like every trial we hold, there is always something that had to be there for whatever it was come to a head, even though they look innocent." Scout asked him what had happened. "Nothing, but she told me this great story to make me remember. A couple was having marital problems. She called the police and had him arrested while he was at work. A possibility of him losing his job, his pension, and anything else he'd gotten while working was something she'd not thought of. She claimed he was beating her, knocking her around a great deal. There were even documents from the hospital to prove she'd been hurt. However, come to find out, it wasn't the husband at all, but the woman's boyfriend. She thought if she were to get a divorce from her husband, she'd get half of his earnings — half of everything, including taking the house. When she found out he wouldn't get jack for being an abusive spouse, she dropped the charges. Humans are very odd, I think."

"That's the story?" Carroll finished up the story, telling him how when she had him arrested at his workplace, his employers had gotten into his computer and found all kinds of child pornography. "So they were both ass hats and should have been put in prison anyway."

"Yes. They were both terrible people, but the man, even though he was innocent of the crime of beating his wife, was guilty of something more serious." Scout asked him how that was pertaining to what he'd asked him. "It pertains to everything. Don't just look at what you're given in any situation. But branch out, think outside the box. At least that's what I got from it. Never look at anything without looking at all of it."

"Okay, I get it. But will you help me look into the gems? And not get me in trouble with your wife? She's very protective of us, and while it's not necessary, it's wonderful having someone other than Mom care if I get my finger smashed or not." Carroll told his brother he was weird. "So? You get to have her with you all the time. However, when she's with one of us, we're the center of her attention. I'm looking forward to having a mate that will look at me the way Hanna does you. It's mushy and very heartwarming at the same time."

"I was wrong about you." Scout thanked him. "You're not just weird, but insane too. How did I not notice that before today? I guess you're better at hiding it. But Hanna has brought it to the surface. Hopefully, she'll let you live with us when the rest of us have mates, and you're sitting in the corner trying to pick up pieces of your insane life while we have fun."

"You're not right in the head." They were entering the kitchen then, and Carroll kissed Hanna on the cheek. "Oh, you're making cookies? I want some too. I'll be good if you promise to give me some to take home."

Carroll went into his office while Hanna told Scout how many cookies he could have. Carroll wasn't worried about not getting any of them. There was his own stash in his bottom desk drawer that he was never going to share with anyone. Taking one out, he began looking up gems as he munched on it, keeping an eye on the door while he did so.

Carroll knew that there were opals and diamonds and that they were raw, not cut. He'd not seen them yet, the pile that had been brought here, but he'd bet they were all beautiful. Not as lovely as his pretty bride, however. Still looking at prices when his brother came to the office, the two of them set to work. Mom was going to join them, he told him, and bring some of the gems with her.

"Good. Because looking at this without reference is not really helpful. We'll need a scale as well as a ruler." He had both in his desk and pulled them out. "This might be more than we can handle on our own. You're aware of that, aren't you?"

"Yes. I thought it would be a simple thing, just looking them up. But it's not. I should have known that, but I was hopeful." By the time Mom showed up, they were more confused than anything. Laughing at their lack of progress, Mom told them she'd find someone she could trust to tell them the gems' value. "That might be better than us fumbling through this."

So while Mom made some calls, he and Scout talked about the calls Hanna was going to make to the Mission family. Something he would have done if asked, but he was so much happier that she was doing it. They'd need a little compassion, and he didn't have it in him to do that with those women. Glad for the distraction of the gems, he knew he needed to get back to work. There was still a great deal to do with the rest of the land they worked.

Chapter 8

Allison hated spending her time in the courtroom when she had so much work to be done at her office. Well, lab anyway. She did have an office but spent less time in it than she did her home. It was a sore spot for her brother, she thought with a laugh, that she worked harder than he did. They'd had a tiff about it last night.

"Because you're a man?" He told her that had nothing to do with it. "Then what, pray tell, has your nuts in a vise about how much I work? You'd rather I was broke and living on the streets?"

"At least then you'd be out of the basement of your workplace and meeting people. When was the last time you were out on a date? I bet it's been months." She didn't tell him she'd been out the Friday before and that it had ended badly for the man. "Allison, you're a young, beautiful woman. I want to see you happy, with a man in your life. Well, not just any man, but one that will be able to get you out and about once in a while."

"Are you happy?" He told her he was, very much so. "Good. I can live vicariously through you." He huffed at her. "I just have it in my head that I'm not ever going to have enough money to keep me cared for when I'm old and gray. I don't care about dating. Men—not you and Tony, but all the other men I know — are intimidated. Some of them are just out for a quick fuck, then never call again. I can do that shit on my own without a man."

"Allison Mission. What a thing to say." She told him it was the truth. "I know you can, and more than likely do, but I don't want to know about it. Tell Tony. That'll embarrass the hell out of him. Do it when he gets here."

They had fun the rest of the night. And Tony, her brother's husband, was right there with her on the fact that men were idiots and wanted only a quickie. She had her own set of rules when it came to dating and men, and so far, everyone had been sorely lacking on about all the points she had.

When she heard them call her name as an expert witness, she stood up. Allison had nineteen such cases today, and she wasn't going to waste any time fucking around with the defense side of the table. Not that she cared one way or another who she was working with, but this guy, Lance Jackson, was one that she had disliked from the moment she came into the courtroom an hour ago.

After being sworn in, she opened up her tablet to the right file. Of course, Lance had something to say about electronics in the courtroom, and she had to show the judge that not only was she not on the Internet, as Lance was accusing her of, but she had all her files for today where she could get to them.

"I guess the morgue is set up much differently than when I was there. I worked my way through college by being a MedTech that would retrieve bodies." She only stared at him, something she'd learned right from the start. Only ever answer things from an attorney that was in the form of a direct question. Otherwise, you were screwed. They'd lead you down a merry path, and you'd be so messed up by the time they were finished that they'd have you thinking you did the murder and were out on the grassy knoll in November. She waited for him to get to his point.

"Dr. Mission, you said you were a doctor. What sort of doctor?" She listed the medical degrees she had. "You must have been a child prodigy then. I've never met someone so well qualified before."

She continued to stare at him. When he turned to the judge, asking him to make her answer the question, she looked at him too. This might be the highlight of the day, she thought.

"He didn't ask me a question. Stating that I might be a prodigy isn't a question. Not to mention, it has nothing to do with my being here today." The judge looked at Lance when she did. "Ask questions or not. I have a busy schedule today, and you're not helping."

"Are you a child prodigy?" She said she wasn't a child at all. "Christ, you're going to be a pain today, aren't you?"

"Yes." She held onto her laughter when the judge laughed too. When he didn't scold her for being honest, Allison decided she was going to have a great deal of fun today after all. Waiting on Lance, she looked down at her watch to see what message had come in. Her brother and Tony were sending her emojis of happy faces. If they only knew how happy she really was.

"All right, Doctor, what were your findings on case number sixty-seven?" She referred to her notes, then told him what she'd found. "Was it murder?"

"I'm not qualified to answer that." He asked her why not. "I'm only the coroner in this. I don't determine the outcome as to who might be guilty or not."

"I see. So what you're telling me is that you don't know anything about this case other than the body of the man you worked on." She only stared at him. "What is it you do there, Doctor? Besides thinking up ways to make sure you aggravate the attorneys that work with you."

"My job." She looked at the judge. "Is this going

anywhere, sir? I mean, he's already insulted my work ethics, disrespected me on what I do for a living, as well as tried to make me answer questions that have been answered. Several times."

"You're right. Mr. Jackson, either get to the meat of why you're here or sit down. We, as she's pointed out to you several times, have a full docket today, and you not understanding what she's here for is getting on my nerves as well." He looked over at her. "Doctor Mission, will you please tell us your findings on the body that we're all here to talk about?"

Reading from her notes, she told them what she'd found. Also that the toxicology report was still pending. For fun, she even told the courtroom what she'd found in his stomach, as well as how long it had been since he'd eaten food. The lack of responses from the attorney didn't matter. She'd been asked to tell them, and she was doing that.

"How long do you think he had been dead before being found?" Allison gave them an estimation on it. Lance, of course, wasn't happy with that. "I would think with all your education, you'd have a better idea than just an estimation."

Nothing from her. But she did want to point out that he'd not know at all if she was not there. When he huffed again, she smiled at him. That, of course, sent him on a rant about how she was purposely giving him a headache.

"All right. I give up. Whatever she's holding back from me is beyond anything that I can deal with. I'm finished with this person." She looked over at the other table, sure that this attorney was going to have the same fun with her.

When he stood up and smiled, Allison thought she could easily lay at his feet. It was that good. Clearing her throat, waiting on him to speak, Allison glanced down at her notes. She didn't want to be caught drooling on her tablet over a man that would more than likely be pissed off before she gave him what she'd gathered for this pretrial.

"Doctor Mission, why is it hard to determine what time Mr. James died?" She told him he'd been lying in the sun for several hours, and decomposition had been rushed. "What, if anything, would that do to a fresh body?"

"The breakdown would have been quicker. Also, any kind of wounds that might well have been on the body before it washed up on the shoreline would have been a place where insects or any other kind of animal would have been able to smell." He asked her, in her estimation, how long the body had been dead. "Anywhere between forty and fifty hours."

This man knew what he was doing. He never once insulted her but asked simple complete questions. She was able to let him see pictures she'd taken when he asked, as well as some of the wounds she would have associated with water damage. In less than two hours, they were moving on to the next case. Allison had a break and was out the door before anyone else.

Just as she was sitting at one of the many tables outdoors for lunch, the other attorney asked if he could join her. When she nodded, he put the largest sub on the table and sat down himself. Before she could comment on how much she was enjoying working with him, he spoke.

"My name is Marley Golden. I'm a last in line substitute for the man who was supposed to be in the courtroom working with you today." She nodded and told him what her full name was. "I have several messages for you from my family. It was only my intention to come here and tell you what I knew, then move on. But I was asked by my boss to come here and work with you on that case. I'm sorry. I'm telling you a lot of information, but I wanted you to know exactly what I was doing."

"I see. Well, not really, but I'm guessing you're going to get to that." He nodded and told her he was sorry. "It's all right, Mr. Golden. I'm sure you are a good attorney despite being a little sneaky. What is it you have to tell me?"

"Your mother was Rachel Mission, correct?" Allison looked around to see if she was somehow lurking in the area. "I'm sorry to have to tell you this, but she died several days ago. Massive stroke brought on by stress and her diabetic illness."

"She's really dead." He said she was, then handed her a clipping that must have been in the newspaper. "I'm not going to tell you I'm all right with her being gone, but I think you might well have already figured that out."

Reading the obit, she was glad to see that neither hers nor her brother's name were mentioned in it. Asking him if she could send it to her brother, he let her. She laid the clipping on the table and took a picture of it with her tablet. Sending it to her brother and Tony, she wasn't surprised to hear from him almost immediately.

"She's dead? How the hell did you find out?" Allison told him she was going to put him on speaker and introduced him to Mr. Golden. "I'm not at all surprised that she had a stroke. She was always bitching about how we needed to do things for her because of her heart. I wouldn't have thought she'd had one, to be honest."

Allison asked Marley what they expected them to do. She had a feeling it was more than him just coming here to tell her about their mother's death. He would want them to come home or something. She wasn't going to do it no matter what anyone said about it.

"There is a will, but I don't know anything about it. I'm sure, like her sister-in-law—who is in jail, by the way—she didn't have too much to say about her children. Did you know that Blanche has a daughter?" Butch told Marley they knew her, and if he wanted them to, they'd get in touch with her. "Please do. I'd like to know if she has any intention of going back to Ohio or not. I'm sure, after hearing the two of you talking, that neither of you will be there either."

"No." She and Butch answered Marley at the same time. But it was her that continued. "We left home and vowed never to return. It wasn't as bad as a lot of kids have it at home. It was especially bad for Meredith, Blanche's daughter. She was older than us and let us live with her until we got up on our feet. Our mom treated our cousin much worse than she did us. At least we had food on the table at least once a day, as well as groceries in the fridge. Meredith would have starved if not for Butch and I helping her out."

"Blanche told my sister-in-law that her daughter wouldn't come home to see her. She said it was her fault." Allison thought that was a lie, but didn't blame the man for relaying what he'd heard. "Is there anything I can do for the two of you? It's at my disposal to help you in any way you need or desire."

"I can't think of a thing. How about you, Allison?" She told them both that she didn't know what it could be either. She was happy to know her mother wasn't around, but she'd not wish death on her. "That's sort of the way I'm thinking. While I had washed my hands of her years ago, I wouldn't have wished her to die like she did. But then, stranger things have happened. I want to thank you for coming out here, Mr. Golden. It was very nice of you and your family to find us and let us know."

"It was actually my pleasure. Your sister is a hell of an expert witness." They all laughed, and Butch hung up, telling her he'd talk to her later. "What do I tell them about the will if you or your brother are mentioned in it? I'll do whatever you wish."

She ate some of her salad before answering Marley. Allison had no desire to go there for any reason. But she'd rather go than to have Butch go. He was still having a hard time telling people he was in a same-sex marriage, something that few knew about him. Finally feeling like she should say something, she shoved her plate away and looked at him.

"I'll go if they can make it so it's only me. Butch would go too if it came down to it, but I'd rather him not to have to. He's saved me a few times—this time, I'd like to save him from what he might encounter back home." Marley asked if it was because of him being gay. "Yes. For the most part, he's had to hide his true self away from everyone. Butch is finally getting to the point where he can introduce Tony to people. I don't want anything to make that go away for him."

"I wouldn't either. He seems like a very nice man,

and I'd want what is best for him as well." She didn't know if he was mocking her or not, so she said nothing. "You're not at all like I thought you'd be. After you giving Lance a hard time, I thought for sure your 'only questions get answered' rule was going to be in your personal life as well. I did love that you had him chasing his ass a few times. It, if you ask me, is a good way to deal with attorneys. Never answer what you don't have to."

"Thanks. When I first started out, it was hard for me not to fill in the quiet time they would give me. Twice I hung myself by giving away too much. I actually learned how to do that from my brother. Butch is the best kind of attorney. Unreadable." She laughed. "I have to admit, it was pleasant talking to you there. You know your stuff as well."

"I'm a great deal older than I look and have had plenty of practice." She didn't ask him but knew somehow that he wasn't lying to her about being older. He had an art about him that told anyone speaking to him that he didn't let things ruffle his feathers anymore. That would only happen with age.

Making her way across the street to the courthouse again, she wondered what it would be like to have a normal life. People had been telling her for years that her upbringing had made her what she was. Allison no more believed that than she did most things people said to her. Sitting in one of the chairs that had been reserved for witnesses, she was disappointed to see that Marley wasn't there. She wouldn't have been either if she didn't have to be.

However, just as the courtroom was being called to order, he came in and sat in one of the few vacant chairs. It was scary to her that she felt safe with him there. Some kind of non-human vibe, she thought and concentrated on the things she had to say in the next pretrial.

~*~

Hanna was next in line to be searched to enter the station. After signing her name to the form she was handed, she waited to hand the clipboard and paperwork to the man in charge of visitors. She had also brought a few things in that Blanche had asked for and hoped that all of it was going to make it to the other woman. Handing off the clipboard, the man stopped running the wand over her and looked at the paperwork again.

"Miss, you're going to have to see the warden." She told him she would do that, and he nodded to the cop on the other side of the room. "I'm assuming that something is wrong. Do I need to call my husband or anything?"

"No, ma'am. I think you're going to be just fine." She was taken to a smaller room than she'd been in previously and asked to have a seat. The warden, his name was Jason Block, came in, telling her how sorry he was that she'd had to wait.

"I'm fine. What's happened?" He nodded and told her why she'd been brought in here. "I see. Why wasn't anyone called to be told that Blanche died in her sleep last night? I mean, I'm the person that should have been called. I'm on the list."

"Truth be told, Mrs. Golden, we didn't know until she didn't show up for breakfast. She's not doing any hard time right now, and the fact that she wasn't down for breakfast didn't raise any alarms. She's been skipping meals since she's been here. But when someone went to get her about your visiting today, that's when she was found."

"Is there going to be an inquiry about her death?" He asked her if she thought there had been foul play. "No. But I'm talking to Rachel's family right now, and if they ask me, I want to have answers. It matters little to me. I'm assuming she didn't call out or anything."

"Not a peep from her since the first time you came to see her. I mean, it's only the second time you've been here, but after that first one, she seemed to settle down and figure out her lot in life." She nodded, knowing it had been hard on the other woman thinking about her lack of family close by and not being able to talk to her daughter. Despite Blanche saying her daughter didn't want to see her, Hanna figured it was just her saying that in the event she did say she wasn't going to come. "I was notified by the funeral home that things have been arranged for her. She's going to go straight to the funeral home from here, then laid to rest next to her sister, I'm guessing."

"Yes, that's what she wanted." Hanna thought about the other things she and Blanche had spoken about. "She made out a will yesterday, I think. Did that get filed? I don't know what she told the attorney she used, but I'd like to make sure that if she had wishes, they are going to be met."

"It's been filed. She asked me the same thing yesterday. Saying that while she didn't have much, she'd like to think someone took the time to figure out what she wanted to be done with it." Thanking him, she also asked him what happened now. "Nothing. I mean, there might still be a trial, but I don't know that. Since she made arrangements for her demise, there will be no more we can do for her from here. You did a good thing with her, Mrs. Golden. Without you, I don't think she would have had such an easy time of it."

"She needed to talk, and I was there to listen, that's all. I was here to tell her that her sister-in-law had passed away, and she asked me to help her out." He nodded, but she could tell he didn't think that was the extent of her helping. Hanna didn't care. She was finished here and made her way to the front to go home. The officer that had taken her to the warden stopped her, giving her the things she'd brought here for Blanche. "You guys should just keep it all. I've been stress baking for three days, and my husband is finally not sneaking cookies out of the kitchen to his office. Do what you want with the other things. Perhaps give them to someone that needs a toothbrush and other personal items."

"Thank you, miss. We'll do that." He opened the tin of cookies and took out one. "Just in case we have to turn it over to the boss. I'd like to know what a real cookie tastes like."

Hanna was still smiling about that as she made her way to the car. Contacting Marley, who was still with the others, she told him what she'd just found out. He said the others could contact Blanche's daughter, and he'd make sure they knew it. Then he asked her about wills.

I know that Blanche mentioned her daughter, Meredith, in hers. Why, I don't know, but she did. The other one, I can find out for you if you give me a second. She reached out beyond where she was sitting to the attorney she knew was in charge of the reading of the will for Rachel. *Yes, both her children are mentioned in the will. The attorney is sending out paperwork to notify them now. Also, you should tell them that while there wasn't much in the way of cash, there was an insurance policy that had been taken out for her when she'd been nothing more than a child. Her parents did it when she was born. The attorney doesn't have any idea how much it's worth, as he's not putting in any effort to get this thing finished up. He's a lazy fuck, and I hope one of them takes him to the cleaners when they get here.*

Marley was still laughing when he told her he'd get back with her later. He was going to have dinner with the Mission family tonight, and he'd been looking forward to it. She told him if he were there, she'd invite him to dinner, and he told her she was spoken for. The ladies tonight, more than one of them, including Meredith, wasn't. He wondered if this is what some people would call robbing the cradle.

I can always dump him for you, if you'd like. They were both joking, and it was fun. But she knew that none of them would ever do such a thing to their brother. She wouldn't either. But it was fun to embarrass them when she could.

Carroll would murder me if I even joked to him about that. Anyway, I'll let you know what I hear later. After tonight, however, I'm coming home. I've got stuff waiting on me, and it's not getting even close to being finished up while I hang out with pretty women. She told him he'd be just fine. *Yes, I know that, but I like to keep busy. You can only walk around this town so many times and know everything there is to know about it. Some of the people too. Nah, I want to come home and sleep in my own small, lonely bed.*

After telling him to have fun, she drove herself home. Carroll was out of town this afternoon, and she had a long list of shit she had to do. One of them was cleaning out the apartment she'd had when working.

That, she knew, was going to take up a lot of her time. If she wasn't so sure she had things there that she'd want, she'd just have a crew go in and donate it all. Carroll even suggested that they go ahead and hire a crew to go in and get it all, bring it here, and she could go through it at her own pace. She knew what that would mean for her—she'd never do it, putting it off in order to spend time with him.

Pulling into the drive not long later, she wondered what it would be like to have so much money that things like too much furniture didn't matter. Wait, she told herself, she did have that now. Picking up her cell phone, she called Morgan. Asking if she and Venetia wanted to have lunch with her, they said yes. Pulling out of the drive again, she scolded herself.

"Nothing is getting done, you know that, don't you?"

But she didn't care right now. Someone was going to make her laugh, and she needed that. Too much had been going on around here lately that made her wish she didn't have any way to contact the outside world. At least she'd have her little bit of world with her family. Hanna knew that was all she needed anyway. If she couldn't go to Carroll for some hugs, she'd get them from Morgan. She was beginning to really like the other woman. A great deal more than she thought she might.

Morgan hugged her as soon as they met up at the

restaurant. Venetia did as well, and Hanna felt so much better. When they were seated, each of them ordering a glass of tea, she told them what she'd found out, also about the reading of the wills. Hanna asked Morgan if she was going to be all right with there not being a trial.

"Yes, of course. She missed, for which I'm grateful, and that's about all that matters anyway. There will be a little more peace around town too, I believe, and that's always a plus." Hanna told her that was a good way to think about it. "I was thinking of something yesterday. Do you know that since you've been living on the property, I've been to town more than I ever had in the previous years? That says a lot for how much I like you, Hanna. You're good for me, I think."

"I was thinking the same thing about the two of you. How much I'm enjoying being around the two of you." Venetia told her how she'd found out she had a sister and let her think it was the police that had found her, not them using magic. The sister, four years older than Venetia, might be able to shed some light on what had happened the night Venetia was kidnapped. "Her name is Zephyrine. I wonder where my parents came up with our names. Not that it matters. I'm just excited to be able to meet her. I wonder why she never thought to contact me."

"We'll find out soon enough. She's coming to town the day after tomorrow. She's been at a school for something I can't remember now, but that time will pass quickly." They all knew what sort of school Zephyrine was in. Wicca. The girl was a witch, the same as her parents had been. Hanna also wondered if she knew where their parents were. She had a feeling that not only did she know, but that she had close contact with them.

Time would tell. With all these women coming here for one thing or another, she wondered if any of them would be mates to her brothers-in-law. Hanna hoped so. She wanted them all to be as happy and having as much fun as she and Carroll were having. Life for her was pretty damned good right now.

Chapter 9

The gems and other pieces that had been dug out of the ground were worth a great deal more than any of them had thought. Once Carroll had laid them out in front of his mom's friend, he had told him he needed to have someone with him at all times that could guard them and him. Asking him why he was surprised by the answer.

"This is well over several million dollars' worth of uncut jewels, Carroll. And I'm only counting the emeralds. There are sapphires here, as well as some really nice-sized chunks of gold nuggets. The diamonds are very nice. However, like everything else in the bag, they need to be cleaned up to see what exactly you're going to be working with. I can't believe you're carrying them around in a zippy bag." He asked him if he'd take on a man for a zippy bag. "I guess you're right. I'd not take you on at all if I was looking to rob someone. Your mother never told me what a big man you were."

Since he wasn't sure how to take that, Carroll asked him about the other items he'd brought with him. Things he'd not known were a part of the dig. To him, they looked like any kind of arrowheads he'd seen in magazines for kids to purchase. However, Doctor Sams said they were authentic.

"I don't know what you mean by that." He told him they were very old and were more than likely as old as he was. "Really? Sheesh. I had no idea. Mom just put them in the bag to see what you could tell her about them. She said to tell you if you wanted any of them, you were to take what you wanted in return for helping us."

"I might just do that, one or two of them. They'll make a nice addition to my collection." While he didn't take any of them then, Carroll could see that he really wanted them all. He'd have to talk to his mom about it after he got an accounting of what he had. "The opals are worth about what I'd think they would be. They'll need someone to polish them up that wants to do it. I'd not let anyone take them all for less than four million on them. There are quite a few of those. The emeralds are large and could be cut down to any size and still be impressive. Those…well, I'm not saying you should hold out for this much, but I'd say at least the four million I said earlier. The gold, about eighteen hundred dollars an ounce. And even if you took out the other minerals surrounding them, you still have about two pounds of it."

Quickly adding in his head, he could understand why Doctor Sams had been surprised by his method of carrying them around. He told him the other gems, while very nice and worth a great deal, still needed to be cleaned up to make a better impression on someone.

"How would I go about selling them off?" Doctor Sams asked him if he wanted to sell them as a lot or individually. "Whatever gives us the most money. My brother is going to use this to open up a secondhand store for appliances. Mom thought it would go a long way to getting him well stocked up."

"I'm thinking he could open himself a new appliance store and not even have to worry about income for a while. Yes, I'd sell them as pieces. That way, you'll get people wanting individual pieces to use rather than the entire lot." Carroll asked him who he would recommend. "I'd say go to an auction house that specializes in this sort of sale. A bigger name place is going to bring in the heavy buyers."

He'd taken notes, thankfully, or he was sure he'd not remember everything he'd been told and advised on. Just to think there was more than enough money in the gems to give each person in town a new washer and dryer, with money left over, made his head spin. It was just things that were dug up from the ground, he told himself. He wondered what other treasures they'd find if they were to do the same thing. Having protection on that part of the land was more important now than it had been before. Christ, he wasn't going to leave the place if he didn't get someone there to watch over it.

Mom, of course, was happy. Not only did she think Sams was right, but she was happy he'd suggested they do this without anyone knowing who they were. She told him to set up whatever they needed to get it started and that she'd help if he needed her.

After working with the auction house Sams had mentioned, he had it all set up for two weeks from today. They could have had it within the next few days, but the place wanted to advertise it heavily, as uncut gems didn't come around all that often. He and Hanna were going to travel to the area they'd been found in to see what else they could figure out. There had to be more than just the items they'd gotten. Besides, he thought it might be fun to be out in the open with her for a few hours.

Carroll worked on the lists he had on the flight home. There wasn't really much for him to do with the gems, so he worked on other things to keep his mind off what was going on around the rest of the town. They'd found out that two homes were going to be auctioned off, and his mom wanted him to be there to get the land. Not because she wanted the dirt, she'd told him, but they could use the houses for the visitors they were having come in. The women, she meant.

I've heard from Butch and Allison. They're both coming here, together with Tony. I think they're going to be surprised about how much no one cares what they do in their own home. It'll be nice having so many around the table. Don't you think? He told her what he thought about one of them being a mate to the brothers. *Could be, but I'm not going to think about it. They're coming here and seeing what sort of shit their mother left, and I'm all right with that. Even Meredith is going to come around. I think all of them were going to come anyway, but having their mothers gone made it an easier decision for them. I know it would have me.*

We should have a hoe down. She asked him what century he was from and then laughed as hard as he'd ever heard her. Having others around for her seemed to be making her not just happy, but he would bet healthier as well. *Roast one of the pigs or something like that. Have some tables spread out, as well as a few blankets. We still have all that firework stuff we had from years ago. Perhaps we can shoot them off as well. Have some real fun.*

I like that idea. It's been a very long time since we've had any kind of community fun. I was just telling Hanna how much more I'm going into town lately. I didn't know it was beginning to look like one of those poverty ridden towns. Someone should have said something, don't you think? He didn't tell her they were afraid of her, but she seemed to understand. *I guess I could have been a little more outgoing. But I am now, and I plan on making some sort of difference if I can.*

They talked all the way back home. He was glad for the company, he told her when she mentioned she'd been talking his arm off. She had made the trip seem less long. Telling her he loved her, Carroll concentrated on what he was doing again. Things, he thought, were going much smoother since he'd been taking notes rather than just trying to remember everything.

By the time he landed, he had most of what he'd been working on finished up. Hanna was at the airport to pick him up, and he was glad she didn't mind being kissed like he meant it. When they were leaving, he told her about his plans of going to the dig site, and she told him that was good. She'd wanted to go there anyway.

"I've spoken to Venetia about her sister. Zephyrine is going to come here and meet with her. I don't know what kind of person she is. She's blocking her mind well enough that I can't get in without hurting her. Since I don't want to do that, I'll have to find out about her the boring way and ask her." He laughed at her pout. "Also, I've asked for a crew of faeries and trolls to watch over the entrance points to where the digging was being done. I don't think we'll have any trouble, but I don't want to take a chance on it."

"Mom told me you were taking over the security

part for her. She seemed to be quite pleased with the measures you've gone to just to make sure everything is safe. Including us." She said with her background, she thought she could use a little more of the things she'd seen put in place in larger buildings. "That is wonderful. What else have you found out? I mean about Venetia and Zephyrine's parents?"

"Not much about their biological parents, but I have about the people that raised them. Betty was in on whatever was going on with this kidnapping thing. I'm not sure why, but she had a change of heart about having to watch over Venetia right up until she—"

Carroll turned to look at her when she stiffened in her seat. Pulling off to the side of the road, he waited on her to tell him. Whatever it was, it was painful for her. Carroll reached out and took her hand into his. She held tightly to him as she explained what had happened.

"Betty is dead. She was killed by one of the men. Since I didn't know who is who yet, I know their names now. Colton Henderson and Benson Applegate. They were both there when she was murdered. They killed her because she wasn't going to lie for them anymore. The woman suffered terribly in those last few minutes of her life." He told her how sorry he was. "Me too. She wasn't innocent in all this, but she didn't hurt anyone by taking care of Venetia. With their names, I can trace them now."

"All right. Did you want to go home?" She shook

her head and said going to the dig site would be just what she needed. "If you get there and want to leave, just say so. This was just something I thought would be fun for us."

"It will be. I just want to look into the men's minds for a little bit while you drive. All right?" He told her whatever she wanted to do was fine by him. "When I find these men, and I will, I'm going to make them suffer in ways they haven't even thought of yet. You can take that to the bank."

"I believe you. So long as you let me be there at your side when you do it. I'd like to see their faces when they realize they've fucked with the wrong woman." She smacked him on the shoulder, and he laughed. "I don't know if you know this or not, but my cat is terrified of you. He thinks if he messes up, you'll hurt him. I've never had that feeling from him before."

"So long as he protects you when necessary, I'll not hurt him at all. But the moment you get even a splinter when he's on duty, I will make him think the whole wrath of hell is on his ass." Carroll was sure she meant it too. His cat curled around him tightly as if he believed she did as well. "I was going to tell you when we got there, but I've had a faerie fix us up a place to stay out there for tonight. I have food in the car for us to snack on and have for breakfast in the morning. You should have seen your mom when I told her I was buying this car. I think she thought it was going to start polluting the moment I turned it on. I had fun telling her it was an electric car and didn't require gas. She's a hoot—you know that, don't you?"

"I didn't know until you came around. I think Mom has been waiting for you as long as I have. You've made her so relaxed it's hard to realize how stressed she'd been all those years."

Pulling into the area where he thought they were going, he wasn't at all surprised to find not just a large tent but a fire going too. This was what they both needed, he realized. A little time away from all the things going on at the house. It wasn't as if they both didn't have plenty to do, but this was just for them. A home away from home for a few hours. He was pulling out the food when he noticed Hanna was talking to one of the faeries. When she started digging near one of the larger stones, he had to laugh. So much for being a restful evening, he thought.

When she sat down next to the fire with him, Hanna handed him several items she'd found. One of them was an arrowhead. The other two things were nuggets. But these were different than the ones he'd had earlier. She told him what she'd found out.

"The ground is cooperating with me on this little outing. They've spoken to the earth, and it's going to push up the things from his depths. Not everything, I was told. There are a lot of gems tangled up in the tree's roots, and it would be harmful to extract from them. I was also told by the trees that they have a few of the pretty stones in their branches. When they grew, with the gems in their way, they would just absorb them into themselves and grow with them. I've been shown a couple of them. They're very proud of them." He asked her to show him when they went on a walk. "You should know too that the stone here, the larger one, has been holding treasures beneath him for centuries. He isn't hoarding them, but once he sees one just beyond his reach, the earth will move enough that they can be hidden by him as well. They were protecting them for your mom. They love her as much as we all do, for what's she's done for the land here."

"She's done so much for everyone and anything around here. Her parents, did she ever tell you about them?" Hanna said she'd heard bits and pieces of it. Carroll told her everything he knew, including how they'd become her children. "My biological mom was older than most of the breeding animals around here. But since she was safe and kept fed, she was able to have us for the world. We were the very first shifters. And in that, we have powers that other shifters, ones that came after us, don't have. But too, there are things we can't do that they can. Like, I can't change you into one of us. That saddens me a great deal. Mom wanted to be able to run with us as well, but it wasn't to be."

"She told me she wished every day that she'd asked for that to be available to her. She said that, too, it would have been nice to be able for her to have a conversation with Golden when she was younger. They were very close." Carroll said he'd gotten to spend his first year of life with his mom and Morgan together and that he remembered them being like sisters. "I bet. It might well have been harder on your mom had she passed away when you were first born."

"It would have been." He looked out over the fire where they were. "How about we have some fun? I know there is a waterway close to here. We can go there, play around in the water, and perhaps make love on the shore."

She stood up and ran. He wasn't sure what her plan had been, but he let his cat take him even as he stood up. Running after her was a lot more fun this way, and perhaps he'd be able to convince her to take a little of her clothing off every time he found her. Yes, Carroll thought, this was just what they both needed.

~*~

Pacing hadn't ever been anything Zippy took lightly. Roman watched his daughter as she stomped her way from one end of the room to the other. If she put that much effort into anything she ever did, especially spells, he thought there would be a good deal fewer people in the world. Like him, she didn't care much for humans either.

"Did you know she was still alive?" He shook his head, knowing on some level that she didn't really want an answer. Besides, he'd answered her several times since Zippy got the call a few days ago. "I didn't have any way of searching for her. I'd never met her, nor did Grandma, or we would have brought her here with the two of you that day. Christ, this is a royal fuck up."

"You saved our lives by bringing our bodies here. If you had not, we would have been buried, and that would have been the end of us. As it is now, we both have some issues. You don't think you really fucked up, do you, Zippy? We'll all go and get your sister and make up for lost time. Do you think she's magical too?" Zippy told him she saw no reason for her not to be. "I don't know. You seem to be much more powerful than even your mom and I. What if you got everything being the first child?"

"I don't think it works that way." His lovely Victoria came into the room, leaning heavily on the cane she needed to walk. He had one as well but didn't need it nearly as much as his wife did. "Mom, did you have any inkling that Venetia was alive?"

"No. But you have to remember that the first five years or so after we were so abused, just trying to heal enough to get around, I never thought of much of anything but the pain." She looked at him. "We've been given tickets too so we can travel to this house. Do we know anything about the Goldens?"

"They're very wealthy. Cats, I think—leopards. Older than we are by a great deal. And their mother is human. I can't get a handle on why that is, but I'm working on it." Roman smiled at Victoria when she huffed at Zippy. "She's working things out. I don't think we should interrupt her right now."

"I'm standing right here." He told her she wasn't standing at all but wearing a trench in the floor. "Why is it that when you do it, it's all right, but when I pace to think, it's wearing a trench?"

"Because you pound the floor with those tiny feet of yours while I just glide across the floor with grace and dignity." They all laughed, just as Roman had wanted her to do. "We'll all go. If we have to, we'll kill the lot of them off and bring Venetia home. That's all there is to it."

"And the two men that hurt you? That took Venetia away? What will we do to them?" Roman didn't answer her right away, and she glared at him. "I should like to be in on whatever you have planned, Dad. I mean, you're going to need me at some point, right?"

"The people we're going to see, they're going to kill them anyway. I thought perhaps we'd try to talk them into letting us have first—what's it called?" Zippy told him. "Yes, first dibs. I'm not going to let them off easily if you're thinking I will. I thought her dead all this time, and they took that away from us. All of us."

Roman was actually excited about seeing his daughters together. He hadn't any idea what Venetia had turned into, but he knew she'd be as beautiful as her sister and mother. There was no way she'd look anything like him. He was too ugly to put to words, he'd always thought. When they settled down for dinner, Victoria told them she was having their things packed. The plane they were taking was a private one the Goldens had sent just for them. He didn't know why they went to the extra expense, but he was happy he'd not have to share a seat with someone he didn't know. Sometimes he had to stretch out in order for his back to not hurt. He wasn't one to make others suffer for his comfort.

By the time they were eating their dessert, they'd gotten around to the men again. He had worked for the two of them, Henderson and Applegate. It had been an all right job, something to waste some time with. When you were as old as he was, things tended to get boring quickly. But he liked the buying and selling aspect of the job. Then he figured out what they were doing.

Roman had never been one to take drugs. He had to now, occasionally. The pain would get the better of him, and he'd have no choice. The same for his Victoria. When they'd both been shot and left for dead, he'd gotten a bullet in the head and his back while his lovely wife had been shot in the chest. Had his mother not felt his pain, they would surely have been put to ground. They, as witches, couldn't heal under the earth. Why? He had no idea but was forever grateful for his mother's fast thinking.

"Do you suppose they will allow us to take part in the demise of those that hurt us?" Victoria laid her head on his chest when they retired to the living room. "I've been thinking of nothing else but Venetia. She'd be in her twenties by now. So long without any contact."

"I've been thinking of her too. I wonder if she'll be a beauty like you and her sister. Also, magic. Do you suppose she's been told she has it? I mean, we did detect a little when she was first born. Now there is no telling how much she might have." Victoria told him they'd help her no matter what. "Yes. As we would have all those years ago."

Roman thought that was by far the cruelest thing these men had done to him and his family. They'd taken not just their child and nearly their lives, but the time they missed with his child. He knew he'd be able to see her soon, but he also knew he was going to make them pay in ways even his daughter, as strong as she was, wouldn't think of. This was, to him, war.

The next afternoon they were packed up and ready to go. He wasn't sure how they were going to get there, not with all the traffic, but almost as soon as he was thinking of getting them a cab to ride in, a limo the size of a small bus pulled up. It took him several seconds to realize this was for them. The man driving even loaded their belongings in the back of it and held the door open for them to be seated. He looked at Zippy when she opened the basket of fruit on the seat next to her.

"These people are wealthy, you said." Roman told her what he'd been able to find out. "They're good at blocking me from getting into their minds as well. I wonder if it's just me or everyone."

"I've not tried. It seemed to me that they were being very generous with their information, and it never occurred to me to look. What is it you found out?" She told him she had found out they were living on a large spread, and they didn't need to purchase anything, that everything they needed or ate was right there. "That's wonderful to know. What else?"

"As you said, the mother is human, but I can only go so deep into her mind." She bit off a chunk of the apple she'd unearthed. "How much you want to bet this is from their place? This apple is amazing. Here, try the grapes."

They were impressed with the tastes they were finding. The note on the basket told them the fruit had indeed been from their place. He especially loved the water, bottled up in a nice glass bottle with lemons and strawberries. Not a combination he would have thought would work, but it was delicious.

The plane was stocked for them as well. Not only were there sandwiches, but more drinks as well. Roman was so happy that he had no problem when Zippy said she was going to see what sort of poison was in them. When she declared them clear, he wasn't sure if she was happy about that or not. Whatever, he thought. This was the way to treat someone, he thought.

The ride wasn't long, but it was very comfortable. There was staff on the plane that catered to them. Also, he and his wife were given faeries to help them with whatever they needed. Zippy, of course, declined, but he could see her watching the little man she'd turned away.

"I wonder what sort of other treats they have in mind for us." Victoria scolded him for being rude, and Pippin, his faerie, told him they were to stay at the big house. "I was wondering about that. A hotel would have been all right, but this is so much nicer."

"The lady of the house has purchased homes as well. They are for anyone that wishes to stay after the meeting. They are very lovely homes indeed. But she also said if you preferred to stay in the house with her, she will be just as happy to have you around. I think she has been lonely for a time." He asked how that was possible with six sons. "She is very dedicated to the farm, sir. It's good to see her laughing now. I think Lady Hanna has brought about a good change to the mistress."

The plane landed as gracefully as it had taken off. The smoothness of it had him thinking he might enjoy flying a little more if this was the way it was done. When they disembarked, they were shuttled to the main building. Roman began to get nervous. Perhaps, he thought, this was a terrible idea.

"Hello, Dad." He turned suddenly and nearly fell off his cane. The man standing there grabbed him so he'd not fall. Roman then looked at the beautiful woman standing next to him. "You look so different than I imagined. But then I really didn't have to go—"

He pulled her into his arms and hugged her tightly. Roman knew that on some level, he should have said something to her. Perhaps hello or something. But she was there—his little baby girl was there, and she called him Dad.

"Roman, let me have a hug." Releasing her even to her mother was harder than he thought it should have been. But since it was his wife, he thought he could allow her to go to her. "Oh, darling, you look just like your grandma did when she was younger. Zippy, come talk to your sister. Oh my, the two of you look just alike, don't you?"

"Hello." Zippy, being her usual self, was slightly standoffish. But Venetia didn't seem offended. The man with Venetia put out his hand and told him who he was. "I'm happy to meet you, Leslie. You look like you can take on the world. Are all of your brothers as big as you are?"

"Yes. Some of them are actually bigger. I also wanted to let you know that just this morning, I realized I'm Venetia's mate. We're working out some of the finer details. But I want you to know I'm not going to come between her and her family. I want her happy, and being with you is making me happy because she is."

He didn't know how he felt about her having a mate. To him, she looked grown up, but she was still his baby. Not voicing his concerns just yet, he hugged both his daughters. He had family now, and he wasn't going to waste a second of being with them by being worried about a man he'd only just met.

They were going to the house when something occurred to him. He only looked at Zippy but didn't say what had been on both their minds. Roman wondered if Morgan knew his daughters would find their mates here. That was why the house had been purchased, perhaps? He didn't know. Thinking that things were moving just a little too fast for him, he leaned back on the seat and closed his eyes. Searching for some kind of clue as to the outcome of coming here, he came up with nothing more than he'd be as welcome as her own sons were in the house. Roman had to admit, even to himself, that he might just like this Morgan person after all.

Chapter 10

Hanna couldn't help but laugh. Every time she did, however, someone else would glare at her. Who would have thought that so much could change in a matter of seconds? And it had, for just about everyone. When Leslie and the others came into the house, Hanna laughed hard. Telling him what was going on was funnier every time she had to speak.

"All of them?" Hanna told Leslie that so far, it didn't include Shiloh. "They're all here? My brothers have found their other halves? This is just crazy."

But it was true. After Leslie had left with Venetia to pick up her family, Meredith had arrived with her daughter, Piper. She was large with a child. She hadn't wanted to come, but with her due date coming up, Meredith hadn't wanted to leave her alone. Almost as soon as she entered the house, Marley had figured out she was his mate.

After that, others were coming and going, and it had felt for a little while there that she'd have to write it all down. But when Allison and her brother came down from the upper floors, having settled into their rooms, Scout nearly fell over his tongue when he figured out he had a mate as well.

Zippy, taking it hard that someone was there for her, was the last to arrive and the mate to Bailey. It was like having a bunch of lovesick puppies running around while each of them tried their best to cater to the needs of their mates. She didn't know which one was more pissed off about it, however, Bailey or Zippy. Hanna thought they were well suited to each other in temperament and personality.

"So I'm the odd man out." Hanna hugged Shiloh and told him that she loved him anyway. "Thanks. I think. But I know that since these guys have mates, I must have one out there as well. I'm going to be taking notes on what not to do when she comes. This might be a lot of fun for us."

"I'm thinking it's going to be a blast." They both laughed as the others seemed to be standing back and getting the lay of the land. Or, in this case, the way their mates wanted to be treated. "I'm betting by the end of the day, not only will they all be pissed at each other, but the women will be ganging up on the men just to keep them at arm's length. What do you think?"

"That you're right. Who would have thought that getting family together for a funeral and the meeting of a daughter could generate so much? I'm hoping when my time comes, I am just as happy as I am right now." She told Shiloh he would be the happiest. "I hope so. This is almost more than I could have hoped for in the way things are going. Mom must be out of her mind with happiness."

"She's in the kitchen. I think when she left here, she wasn't taking it so well. I'm not sure why, but then when I checked on her a few minutes ago, she was crying. Happy tears. But I think she wants to keep her boys hers for a little while longer." She looked at Shiloh. "You should go in and give her a hug. I'm betting she could use one about now."

He didn't hesitate but left her sitting on the couch to watch the others. When Carroll sat down beside her, she kissed him. Roman and Victoria sat down with them, and they quietly discussed what was going on. It was Zippy that broke the quiet.

"I am not going to be a slave to anyone." Bailey told her he didn't expect her to be anything like that. "Well, I'm not going to be easy. You can fucking bet on that. I don't need a man in my life any more than I need a hole in my head."

"I have a hole in my head." She looked at Roman.

"It gives me fits once in a while. Certainly keeps me off balance."

Reaching up, Hanna touched her hand to his head. When she put out her hand, she showed him the bullet fragment she'd been able to take out. Roman stared at her for several silent seconds before he laughed.

"I'm thinking you and I are going to have a great deal of fun, Hanna. Yes, a great deal of fun. Thank you. Now, if you'd do the same for my wife, I'd give you anything you wish, including my life in servitude." Hanna told him they were family and that she didn't want anything but his friendship. "You have it. But I will look for something to repay you, my dear. You've given me more than I could have hoped for when we got here. My daughters are together and with us. That is the best thing a man could ask for in life."

"Wait until the grandchildren come along." They all looked up at Morgan, who had obviously been crying. "I'm so excited to be a grandma now that I could just bust. Please tell me you're going to stay here. I'm hoping to convince Meredith to do the same, along with Butch and Tony. We'll be the happiest family around."

Roman looked at Victoria, and she nodded. "I believe you have your answer, Morgan. Thank you very much. But I have to admit something. I'm starving. Do you think I could get another one of those apples from earlier? The best thing I've ever eaten."

"You can have all you want." As the three of them, including Victoria, walked away, Hanna looked over at Carroll.

"I went to the doctor this morning. For a check-up for insurance. I'm going to have a baby." Carroll, busy watching Zippy and Bailey argue, suddenly looked at her. "Yep, a little baby to add to this mess. What do you think?"

His roar had her covering her ears. When he hugged her, bringing her over to sit on his lap, Hanna felt a happiness she knew was forever. A husband, child, and family. She didn't think it ever would get any better than this.

"I love you, Hanna. So much." Hanna told him that she loved him as well. "I don't know what I was doing before you came into my life, but I surely look forward to being with you as much as I can. I love you."

"And I love you." She stood up. "How about we hurry dinner along? I'm hungry, and I'm sure it'll be entertaining watching these guys get their shit together. Want to help?"

"I do." Heading to the kitchen, she heard laughter there as well. Tonight when they sat down, she was going to have Carroll tell them their news. She couldn't wait for them to be parents. She was looking forward to raising a lot of children. Especially if they were anything like their father. Hanna hugged Morgan and sat at the table in the kitchen.

She'd always heard that the kitchen was the heart of the home. It was truer in this home when the others, mates too, came to join them for snacks and drinks. They'd get things worked out, she knew it. But she was going to enjoy watching it. A girl had to have some fun, after all.

Before You Go...

HELP AN AUTHOR

write a review

THANK YOU!

Share your voice and help guide other readers to these wonderful books. Even if it's only a line or two, your reviews help readers discover the author's books so they can continue creating stories that you'll love. Log in to your favorite retailer and leave a review. Thank you.

Kathi Barton, a winner of the Pinnacle Book Achievement award as well as a best-selling author on Amazon and All Romance books, lives in Nashport, Ohio, with her husband, Paul. When not creating new worlds and romance, Kathi and her husband enjoy camping and going to auctions. She can also be seen at county fairs with her husband, who is an artist and potter.

Her muse, a cross between Jimmy Stewart and Hugh Jackman, brings her stories to life for her readers in a way that has them coming back time and again for more. Her favorite genre is paranormal romance, with a great deal of spice. You can visit Kathi on line and drop her an email if you'd like. She loves hearing from her fans. aaronskiss@gmail.com.

Follow Kathi on her blog: http://kathisbartonauthor.blogspot.com/

www.ingramcontent.com/pod-product-compliance
Lightning Source LLC
Chambersburg PA
CBHW020621180626
46810CB00007B/2881